WISDOM'S KISS

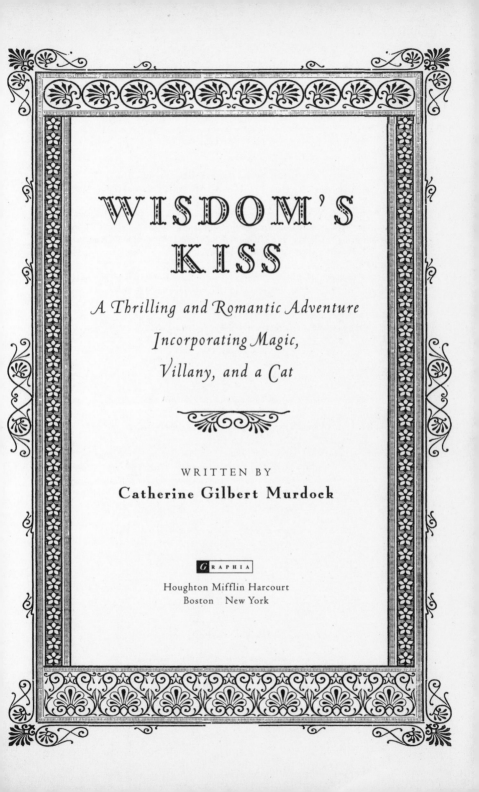

WISDOM'S KISS

A Thrilling and Romantic Adventure

Incorporating Magic,

Villany, and a Cat

WRITTEN BY

Catherine Gilbert Murdock

GRAPHIA

Houghton Mifflin Harcourt
Boston   New York

For information about permission to reproduce selections from this book, write to
Permissions, Houghton Mifflin Harcourt Publishing Company, 215 Park Avenue South,
New York, New York 10003.

Graphia and the Graphia logo are trademarks of Houghton Mifflin Harcourt Publishing Company.

www.hmhbooks.com

The text of this book is set in Abrams Venetian, Centaur MT, Clois Oldstyle, and Perpetua.

The Library of Congress has cataloged the hardcover edition as follows:
Murdock, Catherine Gilbert.
Wisdom's Kiss/written by Catherine Gilbert Mudock.
p. cm.
Summary: Princess Wisdom, who yearns for a life of adventure beyond the kingdom of Montagne, Tips, a soldier keeping his true life secret from his family, Fortitude, an orphaned
maid who longs for Tips, and Magic the cat form an uneasy alliance as they try to save the
kingdom from certain destruction. Told through diaries, memoirs, encyclopedia entries,
letters, biographies, and a stage play.

[1. Adventure and adventurers—Fiction. 2. Supernatural—Fiction. 3.
Princesses—Fiction. 4. Soldiers—Fiction. 5. Household employees—Fiction.
6. Orphans—Fiction. 7. Cats—Fiction.] I. Title.
PZ7.M9416Wis 2011
[Fic]—dc22
2011003708

ISBN: 978-0-547-56687-0 hardcover
ISBN: 978-0-547-85540-0 paperback

Manufactured in the United States of America
DOC 10 9 8 7 6 5 4 3 2 1
4500390704

To Nick and Mimi

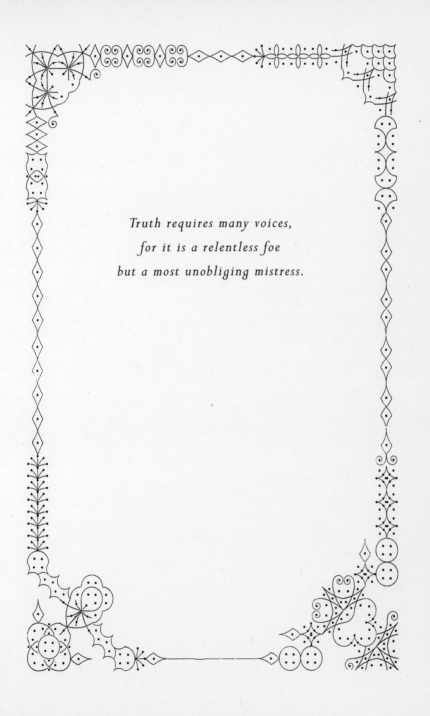

Truth requires many voices,
for it is a relentless foe
but a most unobliging mistress.

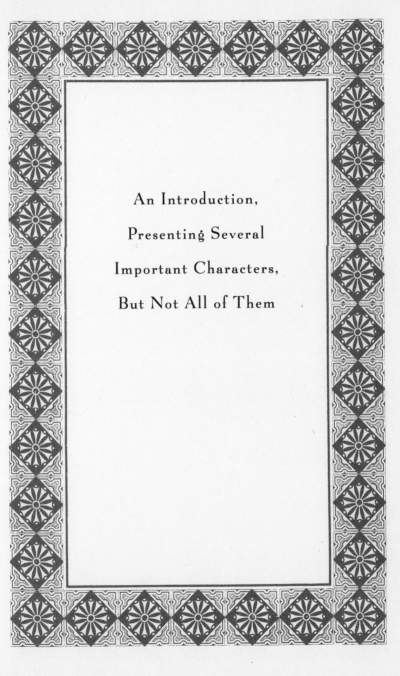

An Introduction,

Presenting Several

Important Characters,

But Not All of Them

A Life Unforeseen

The Story of Fortitude of Bacio, Commonly Known as Trudy, as Told to Her Daughter

Privately Printed and Circulated

RUDY'S SIGHT revealed itself one warm summer night when the child was no older than three.

The Duke's Arms had been lively all evening, denying Trudy's mother even a minute to put her to bed, for Eds made it clear that customers always came first, and Mina was the inn's sole server. Trudy, however, was an easy child, happy to play in a kitchen corner with her yarn doll and tattered little basket, her head a halo of auburn curls streaked with gold. So settled, she did not observe the stranger's arrival or his demand for a meal and a room, and right quick with them both. Nor for that matter did anyone else pay notice to this rawboned traveler missing half an earlobe, for dusty foreigners stopped there daily. Mina was just beginning to serve him when Trudy wandered in from the kitchen, caught sight of the man, and began to scream.

The room quieted at once, and Mina rushed over to take

her away. Yet Trudy stood unbudging. "Go!" she shrieked, pointing at the stranger with one small shaking finger. "Go away! Go away! Go away!"

The man flinched at the clamor, and more so at the two dozen pairs of eyes now focused upon him. He flicked a hand toward Trudy and demanded that Eds take the brat from earshot; this place was supposed to be an inn for God's sake, not a damned madhouse.

That may have been the man's gravest mistake, for while Eds readily agreed about the racket, he abided no criticism of his beloved Duke's Arms. He also knew, with the innate discernment of a successful host, that though this fatherless child meant little to him, she was a favorite with the locals, unlike, say, the miller's youngest son, who—everyone agreed—was a rascal through and through. The regulars who kept the Duke's Arms solvent during the lean summer months were now muttering among themselves, uneasy about this stranger who so distressed their wee sweet Trudy.

Eds thus, without another moment's consideration, ordered him to leave.

"Ye can't toss me out!" the man spat back. "This is a public hostel, it is, and I've nowhere else to sleep!"

"It's my establishment, and I operates as I please," Eds replied coolly. "Besides, I hear tell the heavens make a very fine blanket"—a riposte, it should be confessed, that he had wielded many times, always to widespread mirth. His patrons laughed now, but smiles faded as the stranger cursed Eds and with cold viciousness described his imminent and painful demise. It was only Eds's girth, and cudgel, that got the stranger past the threshold, and no one objected when Eds slammed the door behind him.

Trudy's mother by this time had managed to carry her up to their attic bed, though her wails reverberated through the building. The public rooms emptied soon thereafter, the locals heading home in twos and threes, and in twos and threes they searched their barns and outbuildings before locking every door, so unnerved were they by the child's reaction, and by the stranger's ruthless air. Trudy continued to sob about the awful man "out there" until Mina finally took her outside to see the empty road for herself. The girl peered through the moonlight in every direction and, inexplicably calmed, fell asleep on her mother's shoulder.

Oh, how tongues wagged the next morning, and, oh, how the inn's patrons were teased. What was Eds adding to his beer, the wives asked, that made men fearful old maids? Did a child's tantrum turn Bacio into a village of milksops? Sheepishly the men shrugged, unable themselves to explain their spooked re-action to one ill-tempered customer. Vindication arrived soon enough, for not halfway through morning chores a squad of soldiers rode into town—imperial soldiers, not the duke's preening guards, and their weapons were polished from use, not show. Halting at the Duke's Arms, they asked if anyone had seen a lone traveler, a gaunt man with a severed ear. Eds had only begun to answer when the soldiers wheeled and galloped off toward the pass.

Well. Chores now stopped outright, and pigs and children whined unfed as the good folk of Bacio clustered to gossip over this unprecedented turn of events. Henpecked husbands stood tall, pointing out that their women were right grateful now. Little Trudy, muzzy yet from lack of sleep, received numerous kisses for being the first to notice the villain in their midst.

How much of a villain they did not learn until late that afternoon, when the soldiers returned grimly bearing two bodies: one of their own, who in searching an abandoned shepherd's hut had drawn his weapon too late, and the mangled-ear stranger, whom the squad then set upon and killed at last. This man, the soldiers explained, had robbed and murdered his way across the empire, seeking in particular backwoods inns, and as evidence they displayed the wealth of a dozen victims found in his pack. How had the villagers known to turn him away? For otherwise they'd be burying, not chattering, this sunset.

All eyes turned to Trudy playing tag with the miller's boy. She could provide no explanation other than that the man had "looked bad," and shyly she asked if she could pet the ponies. Smiling, the sergeant hoisted her up to stroke the nose of his majestic warhorse, and over her copper curls he informed the villagers that they owed this child their lives.

Needless to say, the residents of Bacio began observing Trudy, and so noticed that she had a talent for staying out of trouble (unlike Tips, the miller's boy, who would dance on the rooftops like the very devil himself). She was always elsewhere when Eds flew into one of his great rages, and often would coax Mina away as well before the man began seeking targets for his ire. When one day Trudy happened upon Tips and two other boys taunting Lloyds's prize new ram, she begged Tips to play with her instead—to which he readily acceded, for they were the dearest of friends—and therefore the lad was (for once) innocent when the enraged ram burst from his pen, never to be seen again. Yet when young women asked Trudy to prophesy their true love, or Eds sought her opinion of an odd-looking customer, she could only shake her head sadly. Soon, ashamed that she provoked such disappointment, she took to hiding herself away at the approach of any would-be supplicant.

So, they concluded, the girl did have a talent. It was not magic, to be sure—there was no such thing as magic, and any fool claiming otherwise would end up in an asylum, or worse—but a certain limited gift. Tips in his inimitable fashion put it best: "It's simple, really: all the feeling most folks get after something happens, Trudy just happens to feel before." Phrased that way, then, yes, the girl could often see the future, but only her own, and the potential futures of those she loved—sometimes the near future, sometimes not for days hence. But she could not always see enough to avert trouble, and certainly not when it mattered most.

The day the beggar woman limped into town, Trudy, now aged ten, was hanging sheets to dry and so did not observe the woman pass from house to house seeking aid for her sick baby. Nor would Trudy speak, ever, of what her sight revealed when finally she laid eyes on the pair. But from her hysteria, and the sobbing manner she clung to her mother, the residents of Bacio knew it could not bode well. In the days that followed, the deadly fever claimed one life after another, and while some survivors muttered that Trudy should have done more to warn them all, the compassionate pointed out that the girl suffered as much as anyone, and praised how she had nursed her mother without respite until the woman left this earth.

But in truth they rarely paid much attention to Trudy at all. The girl's sight was her own private blessing and her own private curse. The villagers had grief and toil enough, with no time for needless woolgathering. Yes, Trudy was an orphan now with nowhere to go, but others had it worse, others without a pretty face or that mass of Titian curls.

So alone, Trudy had no option but to remain at the Duke's Arms as servant and drudge, her only solace in Tips, who had lost his father in the fever. Such was her life, its cramped bonds of village and labor, and such her life would doubtless have remained forever, were it not for the thunderbolt of upheaval that the world now knows as Wisdom's Kiss.

Memoirs
of the
Master Swordsman
FELIS EL GATO

Impresario Extraordinaire ✦ Soldier of Fortune
Mercenary of Stage & Empire

LORD OF THE LEGENDARY
FIST OF GOD

Famed Throughout the Courts and Countries of the World

&

The Great Sultanate

✳ THE BOOTED MAESTRO ✳

Written in His Own Hand~All Truths Verified~
All Boasts Real

A Most Marvelous Entertainment,
Not to Be Missed!

THIS DAY I WAS TRAVELING SOLO. My latest endeavor had failed, and the great campaigns for which I would become universally renowned were as yet only a promise, though a promise that burned in my breast with unwavering fire. Retaining a powerful memory of the reprobates I had encountered at Devil's Rift, I chose prudence over valor and crossed into Farina via Alpsburg Pass. This route I found delightful in the extreme, for the alpine valleys in the heat of summer present no hardship beyond the cicadas, which crowd the forest treetops in such numbers that their screeching threatens to deafen the hapless traveler. Hardened by the cacophony of war, however, I greeted the buzzing uproar with a cheery smile and, doffing my hat toward their arboreal realm, wished the creatures success in their amorous pursuits.

Thus it was that I entered the village of Bacio lost in my own thoughts and ambitions, and thus would I have departed had I not paused to rinse the dust from my brow in a tributary that flowed aside my route. The residents of Bacio, industrious as ants, had dammed the stream with rocks and earth, creating a pond that fed a mill, the wheel of which turned with inexorable solemnity. I was descending the bank to dip my cravat, my weathered boots almost touching the dark water, when all other notions were chased from my brain by a most extraordinary sight.

Crouched on the opposite shore on the edge of the mill race were two children perhaps of twelve years, a redheaded girl and a boy with hair as sleek as an otter's, each sporting an expression of profound anticipatory mischief. The boy, nut brown with only a scrap of cloth about his middle, kept his eyes locked on the girl's face, his body taut with expectation. The girl in turn focused on the window of the great stone mill abutting the pond. Though I could perceive no activity within the structure, she shook her head slightly, and the boy settled back on his heels. Within a few heartbeats—and much to my surprise at her keen foresight—a scowling young man appeared, his hair dusted with flour. He glared out the window at the children, who feigned ignorance of his presence. The man lingered, doubtless hoping to witness their disobedience; the girl, I noticed, kept watch from the corner of her eye, and after a bit made a slight hand gesture to her companion. What she observed I could not tell, but the sullen man soon after disappeared from sight. Without warning, the boy leapt from his crouched position and landed, balanced as a cat, on the water wheel. As the massive wheel rose, dripping water like a leviathan, the boy effortlessly adjusted his footing on the mossy boards, his arms spread wide; reaching its apex, he launched himself into the air, arcing arrow-straight over the pond. He flipped twice and plunged into the dark water, scarcely raising a ripple.

Breathless as a maiden awaiting her lover did I watch for that black hair to reappear. Never in my life had I witnessed such capability, such physical acumen, in an individual so obviously untrained. That a village imp could conduct himself with so much strength and power left me dumbstruck. Once again, destiny had led me to my El Dorado.

✳ ✳ ✳

The boy—christened Tomas Müller, though in this small hamlet known by the curious sobriquet of Tips—had sprung from a family of loutish millers much as a glorious rose might bloom, most remarkably, in a thicket of thorns. Indeed, the contrast between his talents and his two sulking older brothers reminded me so much of myself at that age that I redoubled my commitment to rescue the boy from this dismal hinterland and present him to the world and the acclaim that were so clearly his due.

Unfortunately, the brothers considered Tomas not so much sibling as slave. The eldest son, who had recently inherited the mill, demanded in no uncertain terms that Tomas remain in their service indefinitely. Emulating in every way the ass that was the second brother's prize possession, the two young men stubbornly declared that he could not depart their workplace for even a day.

Yet again, my singular powers of persuasion were put to the test; polishing my silver tongue, and recognizing all too well that descriptions of *glory* would only set their heels more firmly in opposition, I appealed to the young men's patriotism—and to their purses. Would not the career of a ... soldier—guardian of empire, defender of justice, well compensated in victory—serve the family fortunes? Observing the attention paid my talk of *compensation*, I pressed the point by offering remuneration for their brother's labor. Haggling commenced. For a few gold coins it was determined I would take the boy for my apprentice—as I at that point bore no knighthood, he sadly could not serve as page—for a period of eight years. His future beyond that day would lie in his own two hands. Having no regard whatsoever for the boy's talent, the brothers left the table convinced he would then return to their service, a misconception I made no effort to rectify, as it would have only magnified the price of Tomas's indenture.

Our conference concluded, I stepped outside to find the boy awaiting me, his few possessions in a sack that had quite recently held flour. How he learned of our negotiations I cannot say, as the room was quite preserved from eavesdroppers, but learn he plainly had, for he was now outfitted in stout boots and traveling clothes, a worn cap on his damp locks. His companion, her sweet face marked by tears, clutched his hand, and well could I understand her pain: the boy was already as handsome a specimen of humanity as ever I have observed. Attracting benefactresses, I could see, would not be a problem; the challenge would lie in the delicate deflection of female admirers.

Tomas proffered the girl his goodbyes with a maturity and tenderness that moved my heart; with his every gesture I rejoiced further on the brilliance of my acquisition. Verifying that he would be able to correspond regularly with "Trudy"— indeed, demanding my word and handshake on this matter —he gave her a final embrace and set his pace to mine.

"I am ready," he announced with a most charming gravity, "to begin my adventures."

PART I

SIX YEARS LATER

The Play (As It Were)
Commences

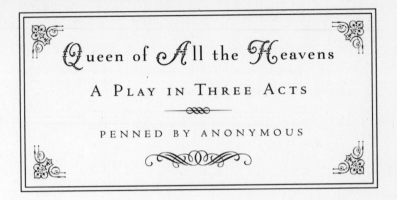

Queen of All the Heavens

A PLAY IN THREE ACTS

PENNED BY ANONYMOUS

Act I, Scene iii.
Terrace, Chateau de Montagne.

An afternoon fete with musicians.
Enter Duke Roger of Farina and Queen Temperance of Montagne.

ROGER: This terrace is lovely, is it not? Your Majesty?

TEMPERANCE: Alas, my poor mother! She adored this terrace. My
sister and I would play here and she, laughing, would applaud . . .
But that was before . . . O woe!

ROGER: Take my handkerchief. Please, consider it a token of my affection . . . [*Aside*] I also mourn for my brother, but life must move
past death.

TEMPERANCE: Were she alive, I would yet be cultivating herba-
ceous shrubberies . . . Now I am obliged to rule, though the throne
holds no magic for me.

ROGER [*aside*]: How can I woo this Temperance? "Queen Melancholia"
is a name more suitable.

TEMPERANCE: And, they say, I must take a husband.

ROGER: Surely some man would tolerate—er, desire you. I myself would delight ... [*Aside*] No! I cannot speak the words! Rather bachelordom and my mother's wrath than this!

TEMPERANCE: Behold—a weed amongst the rhododendrons. I must attend to it ...

Exit Temperance.

ROGER: What a miserable female! What a miserable day!

Enter Princess Wisdom of Montagne.

WISDOM: A miserable day indeed. Your Grace, do not look so abashed! I do not envy you the challenge of courting my sister; 'twould foil Cupid himself.

ROGER: Your Highness. The day grows brighter with your approach, and the very sun slows its descent to linger in your presence ... [*Aside*] If Temperance is melancholia, then Wisdom represents happiness supreme.

WISDOM: Your flirtation is more craft than art—though I am flattered nonetheless. In return I shall tender a confidence: I used to dance upon this balustrade when I was young.

ROGER: Step back! You shall fall and perish!

WISDOM: Your Grace, you are as green as this leaf! I shan't perish: observe how far I lean over ...

ROGER [*aside*]: Such courage! She has pluck enough for two. With her beside me ...

WISDOM: I send this leaf on a great adventure. Fortunate leaf! How I envy you floating away . . . O, I yearn to see the world, yet never once have I left Montagne. Is that not piteous?

ROGER: Piteous indeed, for the world has wonders past counting, and I'd delight in presenting them all to you. But please: I have too little valor. Step away from the precipice or I shall be ill.

WISDOM [*aside*]: "Too little valor"—this I hear too much! All these suitors full of fear. But this one states it at least. And he has a handsome face . . .

ROGER: Your Highness—I am overcome. I fall to one knee to beg your hand in marriage.

WISDOM: To see the world is the richest of offers! Yet you mock me, Your Grace. It is my older sister you desire, not me. Farina has far too much ambition to wed a princess in lieu of a queen.

ROGER: 'Tis true my mother sent me to garner a kingdom with my bride. But with brave Wisdom beside me, I know I shall sway her otherwise. My life rests on this moment. Say the word and I shall be the most blissful of men.

WISDOM: I cannot resist such promise . . . Yes, Roger. Yes.

The Gentle Reflections
of Her Most Noble Grace,
Wilhelmina, Duchess of Farina,
within the Magnificent Phraugheloch Palace
in the City of Froglock

The idiotic buffoon!

The <u>second</u> Montagne daughter! That is the ninny to whom he has promised his heart, and a miserable yellow heart it is—for all the beatings I administered, he remains a coward.

Yet he steadfastly refuses to concede his error—or revoke his proposal!

If only I had another to replace him—would that my firstborn had not perished!—and that the third had never been born, for <u>he</u> refuses even to <u>answer</u> my letters, no matter how often I demand it.

How many times have I explained to Roger (better to have dubbed him <u>Ignoramus</u>!) that we have a plan to which we must adhere?

One cannot take the imperial throne as a lowly <u>duke</u>—we must be <u>kings</u> to manage this—and that title comes solely via <u>marriage to a queen</u>—which that idiot <u>Wisdom</u> most certainly is not!

Although—Montagne, with all its bleatings about feminine parity, may yet be turned in our favor.

The fact that <u>Princess</u> Wisdom does not occupy the throne means only she does not occupy it <u>yet</u>—her listless sister <u>Temperance</u> is all that blocks her way—

I must muse upon this most artful course of action . . .

THE IMPERIAL ENCYCLOPEDIA OF LAX

8TH EDITION

*Printed in the Capital City of Rigorus
by Hazelnut & Filbert, Publishers to the Crown*

MONTAGNE

The Kingdom of Montagne is the oldest continuously held domain in the Empire of Lax, predating by 163 years the establishment of the imperial federation. Unlike its neighbors, Montagne accepted the empire's sovereignty without dispute, joining its mail service, adopting imperial currency, and, with one notable exception, espousing the principles of imperial jurisprudence. That exception is, of course, female succession, a convention the kingdom resolutely maintains despite its affront to every principle of decency and governance. Indeed, the kingdom will even crown a firstborn daughter over younger sons and send its queens into battle, Queen Compassion famously declaring during the Siege of Cheese that "any strumpet can brace a shield." For many centuries the kingdom claimed a connection to sorcery. Virtue, foundress of Montagne, asserted on innumerable occasions that she was a witch, and furthermore that magic flowed in the blood of her descendants. Early Montagne historians credited supernatural forces for the kingdom's victories in such battles as the Drachensbett Cloud Wars and the Magnanimous Goat Incident. Within modern Montagne, however, such babble of witchcraft is treated with derision, and its now-rational rulers ascribe past success to geography, military prowess, and not-inconsiderable—if inconsistent—good luck. The kingdom's long-standing pacifism has been repeatedly challenged, most notably by the surrounding kingdom of Drachensbett, whose many attempts at conquest were rendered moot during the reign of Queen Benevolence when Montagne, in a stunning turn of events, absorbed its larger foe.

A Missive From ~Tips~

<s>The Booted Maestro</s>

Dear Trudy,

*~Its been so long I know I shouldve written sooner~ Im sorry I
havent written much in the last months — I didnt think we would
be so busy! But I dont mind because Im making even more ~tips~
money. Felis works us so hard — he must say <u>work harder Tomas</u>
50 times a day! Or he says that hes wasted the <u>last 6 years of
his life on me</u> and that <u>the empire would be far better off if Id
stayed home grinding wheat</u> but I know thats not true + hes just
saying that to make me ~consen~ ~consan~ concentrate. At least I
~think~ hope he is! At least he doesnt mind my using his ~station-
ary~ ~stationerie~ writing paper — maybe thats his way of saying
hes not too cross.*

*I wish I could describe how ~strange~ different the Sultanate of
Ahmb is, the smells + the feeling + the people. Its nothing like
Bacio, thats for sure! Or anywhere in Lax for that matter! Its so
hot here even at night — when I get back from ~work~ guard duty
I cant bear even to light a candle. But today I have a holiday +
Im sitting in the bazaar drinking tea with a bundle of presents
for you + Hans + Jens — I think ~its obvious~ you can figure out
who gets what!*

Im so ~~disappointed~~ ~~upset~~ sorry to hear Hans didnt like the watch I sent, I can just hear him saying <u>why does a miller need to know the time?</u> Maybe someday he will like it. At least I ~~know~~ hope you liked the ribbons! No one here has hair ~~so red~~ your color, if you came here youd have to hide it or the sultan would ~~kidnap~~ ~~steal you away~~ make you one of his wives. I wish I could show you the gift he gave the emperor, its the most amazing thing Ive ever seen—I got to see him give it too, as I was ~~working~~ guarding the emperor that night. His majesty gave him a gift almost as nice: a clock made in Pamplemousse, with 12 gold birds with ruby eyes that sing the time. If everyone got wedding presents like that, Id ~~get married~~ be really happy for them.

You keep asking when Im going to return to Alpsburg + Im sorry but I dont think Ill make it back this year either. <u>Another</u> year, I know, but its ~~for the best~~ so difficult to get away. Please dont be sad. I think of you all the time + hope youre doing well. Im truly sorry Im not able to return. Maybe the fabric will help—~~I know it wont make up for me~~ its the best I can do. Women here—rich women I think from the looks of them—use fabric like this for veils. They cover their faces but you can still see how pretty they are. But no ones as pretty as you—

—Tips

THE IMPERIAL ENCYCLOPEDIA
OF LAX

8TH EDITION

Printed in the Capital City of Rigorus
by Hazelnut & Filbert, Publishers to the Crown

ALPSBURG

A province located in the central mountains of Lax, Alpsburg contains the only navigable pass through the Alpsburg Mountains south of Devil's Rift and is thus essential when the Great River is in flood or ice. The land has been inhabited since ancient times. For centuries autonomous, recognizing the imperial throne, the country was absorbed by the adjoining Barony of Farina after Roberto the Lonely died without issue in Year 3 of the reign of Rüdiger II. Alpsburg produces wheat, lumber, wool, and stone in abundance, although the bulk of the province's revenue has historically been drawn from tolls. The province's former capital, Alpsburgstadt, remains a center of trade, and the village of Bacio serves an important if seasonal function as the western terminus of Alpsburg Pass. The lyric poem "Bacio mi amore" by Rundel of Gebühr describes the peerless beauty of this village, though his words should be interpreted in light of the poet's relief at surviving a late spring blizzard while crossing the pass. The village is the birthplace of the renowned swordsman-artiste Tomas Müller and Fortitude of Bacio, the alleged seeress; and the two, remarkably enough, were childhood friends.

From the Desk
of the
Queen Mother of Montagne,
& Her Cat

To My Dearest Temperance, Queen of Montagne,

Granddaughter, this slog toward Wisdom's nuptials, though not half-completed, has been most memorable — that I can assure you — and if by some blessing I manage to survive it, I shall regale you for hours with tales of our misadventures. I trust you are enjoying your newfound solitude, and I cannot wait to hear of your many successes as queen. As I have droned to you on occasions past counting, the decision to govern must come from within, and without your sister casting her gregarious if irreverent shadow upon the chateau, I know you will thrive as does a flower in fresh sunshine. Please comfort yourself with the knowledge that whatever matters of state might occupy you, they are surely more pleasurable than this trip.

You doubtless recall that our departure from Montagne was without incident, and the barge — quite handsome, freshly painted, with large and comfortable quarters — appeared undeniably regal even to my ancient and jaded eyes. Certainly the farmers and bargemen we passed seemed to think so, and it was uplifting indeed to accept their congratulations and best wishes. If there is any private resentment within our nation, it must be quite private indeed, to judge from the enthusiasm of the citizens — yea, and foreigners — we encountered.

Would I had curtailed my good cheer, for soon enough the fates punished my optimism. One day past Bridgeriver, the river was running so high that we feared to remain aboard our vessel, and only then did we learn that the spring rains, while abundant in Montagne, have been of historic and terrifying volume in greater Farina and that Devil's Rift was therefore navigable only to madmen. Why our pilot, hired in Bridgeriver, had declined to reveal this critical piece of information I cannot imagine, for the gold he hoped to gain for his service was most certainly not forthcoming. Our royal ancestors would have taken much pride in the lashing I gave the man — only with words, though had I possessed a crop the punishment would have done credit to a boatswain. In any event, thus stranded in the forests of Pneu, we were forced to return to Bridgeriver by foot and farmer's cart (pig farmer, should you desire that olfactory detail), our trunks in a precarious and swaying heap. Nor was the riverfront inn in which we spent the night quite of Montagne's standards — I fear the ladies Patience and Modesty were quite decimated by bedbugs, or so it appeared the following morning.

At last we arrived, again, in Bridgeriver, where it took all our efforts to acquire a vehicle for crossing Alpsburg Pass. Given that their requirement of tribute has increased with every annum, the fine residents of Bridgeriver lose no love on the Duke of Farina, and fretted not at all that they were delaying the man's union with his betrothed. After two days of negotiation — the mayor of Bridgeriver puts to shame the haggling of every wool merchant I might name — we acquired a carriage and set out. Last night we sojourned in the manor house of the Baronet of Savory, a most ill-suited name given that the dinner he served would have disappointed a prisoner. Tonight — our last in Pneu, I dearly hope — we shall stay in the mountain hamlet of Frizzante, which I hear tell contains an excellent tavern, and a treat it will be to dine as I am so indulgently accustomed.

Dizzy — or <u>Princess Wisdom,</u> as the Baronet of Savory insisted on calling her ad nauseam, lingering each time over <u>Princess</u> — to my relief has demonstrated only enthusiasm for our journey, an energy that bodes well for her future in Farina. Escoffier as well has served as a most satisfying companion; it helps that unlike this stout old lady he can be easily toted when he wearies. I wish you could have observed the cat glowering at the baronet, so disappointed in the paucity of the meal that he looked quite prepared to put the man on a skewer and roast him for dinner. I made sure to keep my friend close at hand lest he attempt what he should not. I declare, I occasionally wonder if our past connection affects us yet, as Escoffier at times behaves as though he believes himself in possession of hands and nimble fingers, while I on entering our chambers last night detected the scent of mice—and my heart sped at the promise of pursuit! You may be certain I did not act on this hankering, however.

Enough! I drone on, and the carriage is at last ready to depart—why the ladies feel it necessary to primp for a day of passing sheep meadows, I cannot understand. Soon enough, I trust, I can return to Montagne and your side. I know how heavy the crown weighs upon your young head, and how you mourn the premature suspension of your studies. But inscrutable Fate has ambitions for us that we cannot possibly comprehend. The death of your mother—my daughter—is the greatest tragedy of my life and a burden I will bear forever. We must strive, however, to shoulder the responsibilities thrust upon us with the eager determination that she would expect.

With that in mind, I shall scrutinize every bachelor in Froglock and return to you with a list of names ranked by their professed interest in, and knowledge of, horticulture. We shall find you a mate, my dear, one who will delight you as much as your father did your mother, and my Florian did me.

Your doting grandmother,
Ben

THE SUPREMELY PRIVATE DIARY
OF ~~WISDOM~~  OF MONTAGNE

Any Soul Who Contemplates Even Glancing
at the Pages of this Volume Will
~~Be Transformed into a Toad~~
Suffer a Most Excruciating Punishment.
On This You Have My Word.

Tuesday—

I cannot believe these people! I finally get to see the world—only to find myself encumbered with a veritable battalion of worrywarts & fussbudgets! Nonna drones on as if we were starving—the food is not spectacular to be sure but we are certainly in no danger of famine. And the Sprats as I have taken to calling our l-in-w (it is unfair to call Lady Patience "Jack Sprat" as the fellow in the rhyme never complains—but Lady Modesty v. much matches the dimensions of his dame!)—the Sprats almost had hysterics over a few tiny insect bites tho I could barely see the marks not that they value my opinion. And our secretary sees highway robbers at every turn & wrings his hands if we're even five minutes late. Well we're a lot later than that now! But so what? This is more adventure than I've ever had in my life & probably more than they've had all put together.

Yes that inn had mattresses older than Nonna Ben but I could see the river from my room & hear the boatmen—who know more curses than I shall ever be able to remember! One man in particular had a true gift—wouldn't it be wonderful if I could rattle off blasphemies so! He was a veritable poet—I could have stayed awake until dawn just to hear him! In fact I was wholly primed to smuggle myself down to the dockside bustle that I might better attend when Escoffier appeared quite glaringly on the windowsill relaying with every black whisker of his being that if I so much as stepped from my chamber I should be in Very Great Trouble. How he knew to materialize at that moment I can't imagine—Nonna Ben has vowed never again to link with him and means it with all her soul—nevertheless E must have some grandmotherly residue yet within as he is cleverer than ever a cat could be—too clever for my taste as I have chaperones enough as it is! So alas instead of strolling the docks incognito I was forced to pass the night perched at the window like a trapped princess (which of course is precisely what I am at present much as I may delude myself otherwise) listening from afar. At least E kept me company in his furry way.

I am sorely tempted to test my boatman vulgate on the Sprats who v. much deserve it as they complain so much—have they never ridden by carriage before? Of course we have to walk up the hills! The horses aren't mechanical devices—they have enough work just to drag all that ridiculous finery—I even explained to Jack Sprat that if she hadn't insisted on packing half the castle wardrobe she'd probably be able to ride—which she did not appreciate at all!

I was about to tell Mrs. Sprat that her walking was more helpful than Sprat & I put together as she weighs more than Sprat & I put together but it was clear the jest would fall short—instead I simply joined the horses & the coachman who is far better company than they & who is teaching me to spit—we make sure Nonna Ben & the Sprats are far to the rear before we practice! In return I am teaching him cartwheels altho he's too old to start—I think he asks simply because he enjoys watching me show him—it's great fun to demonstrate—he's amazed my skirts never once fall up—or would it be fall down if I'm upside down? But I'm so v. quick I remain a proper lady throughout—not that I'd ever let the Sprats appraise my behavior!

We are traveling now through mountains almost as high as Montagne's—we have to walk—& practice spitting!—almost all the day! I believe we're a week late at least—I've given up listening to the secretary's assessments as his every calculation forecasts calamity—but I don't care one dried-up old raisin! I've the rest of my life to be a wife—how many other opportunities will I have to experience such a delightfully wayward journey?

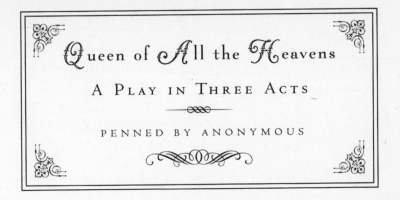

Queen of All the Heavens

A Play in Three Acts

PENNED BY ANONYMOUS

Act I, Scene v.
Interior, Frizzante Tavern.

Morning. A great spread of food.

TAVERN KEEPER: It is the dream of my life to serve a queen— particularly one so receptive to the culinary arts! This meal shall be remembered forever . . .

Enter Benevolence carrying Escoffier, and Wisdom,
Lady Modesty, Lady Patience, and others.

BENEVOLENCE: Good morn to you, my fine man. What glories have you prepared us? I vowed after last night's feast I should never eat again, yet my sable companion and I find ourselves ravenous once more.

TAVERN KEEPER: My chefs toiled through the night . . . I have for you fine omelets, sweet pastries, and my personal masterpiece: oysters.

PATIENCE: Oysters! What a tremendous delicacy! O, they taste divine!

MODESTY: The crust so delicate—the interior so creamy . . . I believe I shall have four if it does not appear too greedy.

WISDOM [*aside*]: That is a spectacle well worth forgetting . . . This roll is still warm. I am quite content with it alone for the moment.

TAVERN KEEPER: Your Majesty, you do not dine? Are the oysters not quite to your satisfaction?

BENEVOLENCE: My friend turns up his nose—this cat knows more of cookery than most men.

TAVERN KEEPER: These oysters arrived only this morning, packed in ice . . . I could not resist their purchase, however dear, as I knew my guests deserved the best.

BENEVOLENCE: Of course you shall be justly compensated. But when traversing mountains, I prefer mountain fare. I recall a leg of lamb that left last night's table only half-consumed . . . Wisdom! You cannot depart so soon! You have barely swallowed two mouthfuls!

WISDOM: There is a man outside juggling! That entertainment is all the nourishment I require.

Exit Wisdom.

BENEVOLENCE: His Grace will find it quite the chore to tame his feral bride . . . Come, Escoffier, let us break our fast. Truly this meal will never be forgotten.

THE IMPERIAL ENCYCLOPEDIA OF LAX

8TH EDITION

Printed in the Capital City of Rigorus
by Hazelnut & Filbert, Publishers to the Crown

ESCOFFIER OF MONTAGNE

The history of the Empire of Lax would not be complete without the chronicles of its most revered pets: the elk-hound Steadfast, whose life was immortalized in the ten-hour opera *Paws of Honor* (performed only once); the poodle Brownie, who in mistaking approaching soldiers for tree squirrels alerted Castle Underjoy to the imminent attack; the Pekingese Darling, who inspired the foundation of the Darling College for Women in Gebühr. None of these canines, however, matches the cat Escoffier, the only animal ever to be awarded the Medal of Lax for service to empire. His life story, much altered and embellished, may yet be found in fairy tales, and his visage observed in the black-cat emblem of the Imperial Department of Revenue. Born in a granary in Montagne, the mongrel was adopted while still a kitten by Benevolence, the elderly queen mother, in yet another example of that kingdom's peculiar eschewal of pedigree. His name derived from a famed chef, as the cat's appetite and tastes were legendary, and visitors to the royal seat learned to disguise their shock at the spectacle of queen and cat dining together at every banquet. Escoffier accompanied his mistress on her travels throughout the empire. He appeared to be unsettlingly cognizant of human speech, and his tendency to appear at occasions of portent—often without his mistress—led more than one unnerved observer to declare him bewitched. This accusation Benevolence contested most heartily, fearing for her pet's life, and in several royal proclamations declared that he was only a cat, and a lazy one, to boot.

A LIFE UNFORESEEN

THE STORY OF FORTITUDE OF BACIO, COMMONLY KNOWN AS TRUDY,

AS TOLD TO HER DAUGHTER

Privately Printed and Circulated

POOR TRUDY was caught by surprise while attempting again to retrieve Soots.

The old fowl insisted on nesting under the gorse bush across from the inn; that her chicks remained unscathed after two weeks so encamped was strong testament to the hen's pugnacity, if not her sense.

Still, it did not require the gift of sight to see that one hen could not protect a dozen chicks from all the predators in Bacio or from the interminable spring rains. So Trudy—diligent, solicitous Trudy—found herself once more rooting through the thorns, avoiding as best she could Soots's glare and beak and muttered fowl curses.

"Just come out," Trudy sighed. "If you go back to the henhouse, you'll have food and water and no foxes . . . Oh, baron's brains, I'm talking to a chicken!"

How Tips would laugh at this, if he were here! He'd laugh, but in a kind way, and wriggle through the gorse with no thought to his own discomfort. If he were here now, he and Trudy would be laughing together, just as they used to. Just as they would again, someday . . .

Trudy glanced about with a start. How long had she been staring into space, dreaming of a boy an empire away? Fortunately no one from the Duke's Arms had seen her, for every man and woman was occupied in tending the guests, human and equine, that had inundated the inn since the flooding began. Several local farmers, their fields too wet to plant, had been taken on as hostlers. Their female kin toiled in the kitchen and laundry, though the young women between them hadn't the sense of Soots, and with such featherbrains to manage, Trudy had even less chance to finish her own work. Which, by the way, she should be doing right now rather than tending a family of vagabond poultry. Tending it badly.

She stood, brushing dead leaves from her skirt, and could not help glancing west toward Tips's mill. Not that it was *his* mill; the solicitor had made that clear, as had Tips's brothers and Tips himself. But it would be his someday. How could it not, what with Hans and Jens both childless—not that there was any mystery to that one, nor grief either . . . Tips had to end up with it. Gristmilling was in his blood, much as he'd washed his hands of the flour. However good a soldier he was, he'd be just as good a miller when the time came.

Still musing on Tips's future, and hers, Trudy turned east. No matter how many carts of quarry waste they spread, the sodden road was less highway than riverbed. The mud . . .

Without warning, Trudy staggered backward. Something was coming. Something bad—something very, very sick indeed —was coming down the mountain.

Buckled to her knees, gagging into the mud, she struggled to remain calm. Think, think! How should she respond? What would her mother do? And who—or what—could it possibly be, headed straight for Bacio—and straight for the inn?

From the Desk
of the
Queen Mother of Montagne,
& Her Cat

My Dearest Temperence, Queen of Montagne,

Granddaughter, where to begin! Last night we dined in Frizzante, where the lamb roast was excellent, if not quite on par with Montagne's, though of course I am too partial to judge. Our sleep, too, was quite satisfactory. When shall I learn, even in my dotage, to accept every favorable event with extreme caution, given that it will doubtless progress to disaster? It most certainly did in this case, for the tavern keeper this morning set out a great spread of <u>oysters.</u> Oysters, in mountains yet shrouded in snow! Only Dizzy, myself, and a coachman abstained, though in Dizzy's case it was ungodly curiosity and not common sense that preserved her. Escoffier and I breakfasted instead on the last of the lamb, Escoffier regarding the scraped bone with such longing that I feared he would metamorphose into a hound and drag it off to bury.

Our subsequent trip through Alpsburg Pass I shall never forget, much as I long to; I'd wager the kingdom that no member of our party will ever again dine on oysters. Within two hours of our passage the first guard collapsed from his horse. In the next thirty minutes every man and woman save Dizzy, myself, and — blessedly — our coachman was similarly afflicted; poor Modesty and Patience reclined with their heads hanging from the carriage windows, moaning piteously, while Patience's maid lay curled at our feet in a miserable pile, not that the others were cogent enough to object, or even to pay heed.

Dizzy of course fled the carriage at once. I grant she made herself more than useful by leading a string of horses while the guards drooped green-faced in their saddles, though her exhaustive questioning of the coachman on the art of bareback riding, his encyclopedic knowledge of which she has only recently become aware, demonstrated all too publicly her indifference to the suffering around her. Within the carriage, I kept a handkerchief — perfumed, you may be sure! — to my nose, removing it only to open the door at critical moments and to reassure my companions that they were not facing death, much as they might crave it at that minute. Escoffier dozed beside me, occasionally cracking one eye when the moaning grew too vocal.

When not serving as stopgap nursemaid, I distracted myself from this pageant of wretchedness by pondering how exactly — and when! — we are to arrive at Phraugheloch Palace. Our tribulations have left us seven days overdue at the Farina court; while rational minds accept this as ill fate, you and I both know that Duchess Wilhelmina does not gravitate toward rationality, or charity. As much as I fear the insult — or what she will doubtless take as insult — of our late arrival, I worry still more about the poor showing we will make at the palace gates. Though we of Montagne have little regard for protocol's more obscure constrictions, I recognize that our arrival sans retinue will leave us looking more beggars than sovereigns — which a queen must never allow, particularly when dealing with Farina! Patience and Modesty, and their maids, too, require several days' recovery — days we do not have. If only I could conjure footmen from mice! Fear not; I write only in jest. I would never seriously consider such a hazard. Sorcery would only multiply our quandaries. Perhaps I could dress Escoffier in livery and put him to work, though I'm sure he would fall asleep on his feet — which puts him in league with most castle staff!

Quipping aside, I cannot — we cannot — offend the duke and his mother; how awful it would be for Dizzy to face such prejudice at the commencement of her matrimony! Truly, I am absolutely frantic; our wretched delay, capped by this horrific oyster sickness, has put me in a state of disorientation such as I have not known in years. A solution will come, I am certain, to our desperate short-handedness. But how, or when, I have not a single indication.

At last — the entire entourage with the exception of Dizzy and Escoffier quite woebegone — we arrived in Bacio, at a most extraordinary inn (the sign over the door reads THE ~~ALPSBURG~~ ~~BARON'S~~ ~~COUNT'S~~ DUKE'S ARMS — a history book in one weathered marquee!). There, to my astonishment, we were greeted by a dozen servants proffering buckets and blankets and damp, cool cloths. Lady Patience, the first to alight from the carriage (much splattered, I fear, though dusk hid the worst of it), fell into a swoon that was perhaps not entirely wretched given the strapping young man who caught her; the others were similarly assisted indoors. Dizzy, heaven help us, established herself in the stables, unsaddling horses and chattering away with the hostlers. How the staff knew to prepare for a dozen invalids, I cannot imagine. It was assuredly the most comforting reception I have ever met . . . but so unnerving!

Your shaken grandmother,
Ben

Postscriptum: The Duke's Arms includes on its staff one maid whom I suspect is quite comely beneath her headscarf and homespun; certainly she has a pretty smile when not over-whelmed by shyness, and goes about her duties with envi-able efficiency. Admiring her handiwork this evening, I commenced scheming how to include her in our retinue. If the task of a lady-in-waiting is to flaunt through beauty and breeding the good taste of our court, we could do worse; cer-tainly no worse than our present ladies, who sprawl prone with their heads in dishpans. No sooner had this notion flitted through my mind, however, than the girl turned to me wide-eyed and said, "But Your Majesty, one is born to the position of lady-in-waiting!" Is that not unbelievable?

Post postscriptum: I apologize for droning on so about our troubles; this is your time, and please do not squander any of it worrying about us. Ruling a country is a most formidable responsibility, and too often dispiriting, particularly for one inclined to doubt her own abilities. You are doing so well, my dear; I beg you believe me on this. The chateau must be bless-edly quiet with so much of the court away. Employ this time to spread your wings! Without your butterfly of a sister or goose of a grandmother, you may find your wings stretching very far indeed!

THE SUPREMELY PRIVATE DIARY

OF ~~WISDOM~~ *Dizzy* ∧ OF MONTAGNE

Any Soul Who Contemplates Even Glancing
at the Pages of this Volume Will
~~Be Transformed into a Toad~~
Suffer a Most Excruciating Punishment.
On This You Have My Word.

Wednesday—

When I am ancient & writing my memoirs I shall entitle
this chapter "The Puking Path." Or perhaps "The Retching
Road"—that's more accurate as the Alpsburg Pass is quite
clearly a decent road when it's not full of mud. Or in our case
of vomit. The worst part is that no one else found it funny!
Which it was! It was horribly amusing but I couldn't laugh—as
Nonna Ben is forever repeating, I must strive <u>to present more
graciously my innate compassion.</u> Also Mrs. Sprat would have
smitten me dead. (Perhaps I could call my memoirs "The
Sprats Go Splat.") So I walked with the coachman—he drove

& I walked—thank goodness he was healthy or we'd yet be marooned in that godforsaken wilderness—& I found out he knows how to ride bareback! He can even stand at a canter! With no hands! I begged him to show me but he said it wasn't the proper time. Then once we arrived in Bacio everyone was so busy mopping up that we couldn't. Also it was dark by then.

There's a girl who works in the inn here who has the most spectacularly beautiful hair I have ever seen in my life. If I had hair like that I would keep it long & loose & not even bother with clothes because no one would notice the rest of me! This afternoon when we arrived she wore a little kerchief & then when she came to our room tonight she had it hidden by a v. pretty scarf—even I noticed it & I'm dim as a door knocker when it comes to that sort of thing tho I was careful not to say a word. But then the scarf slipped off for a moment & it took all my resolve not to scream in envy! Her hair is not carroty at all but just lovely red & it has the most beautiful waves ever. The Montagne wig maker would follow her around like a little lost puppy. I did my v. best not to stare but felt myself growing positively green. She's terribly aware of it you can tell by the way she covered it up at once. Nonna wanted her to travel with us as we are decidedly short of a retinue—a functional retinue that is!—but she said no. So would I in her shoes—with hair like that she doesn't need anything else in the world. Certainly not waiting upon this gaggle of gaggers. Nor would I wish her to join us for my own mousy locks do not come close to hers—& I shan't even begin to describe the difference in our figures!

At least Nonna is diligent—unlike me!—about writing to the Dearly Beloved Sister. Teddy—excuse me Queen Temperance —always complains most intemperately about being left out—I hope that for once she's happy to be somewhere else! Tonight at bedtime I had to help Nonna as no one else could—it makes me appreciate how much work it is to "keep us up" which is a pun on upkeep but it doesn't make much sense the way I put it—there's a joke in there somewhere I think—in any case I made a right hash of Nonna's gown— I had no idea folding was so hard! I'd always thought it'd be absolutely joyous to be free of staff but now I am not so certain—if I am expected to iron or dress hair then we might as well return to Montagne! Normally I would say I do not care about appearance—which I v. much do not!—but even brave Nonna is so fearful of Wilhelmina that now I fear her as well! I know we are royalty—Roger knows—his bothersome mother must know as she sent us cartloads of nonsense to sign—but for all those gallons of ink we must still display our regality to the court!

Just think! By tomorrow night—if we acquire fresh horses enough!—I shall be at Phraugheloch with my betrothed. "The

Duke & Princess of Farina"—an awkward style but at least I can flaunt my princess over that conniving duchess!

Imagine—I am to be a wife.

I do hope I have chosen well.

THE IMPERIAL ENCYCLOPEDIA OF LAX

8TH EDITION

Printed in the Capital City of Rigorus
by Hazelnut & Filbert, Publishers to the Crown

FROGLOCK

Occupying the lowest fording point of the Great River, Froglock has served as a center of trade and defense for a millennium or more. Much of the city's great wealth derives from this ford, and more recently from the twelve-arch bridge built in the reign of Clyde, Baron of Farina. (Entitled by him a "Dazzling and Fitting Triumph," the span is better known by its acronym, the Daft Bridge.) It is not surprising that the city's premier industries—weapons and paper— relate directly to the defense and administration of this bridge, as well as to other tolls throughout the provinces and holdings of Farina. According to legend, the city's name was bestowed by residents grateful to the amphibians that would croak an alarm when nocturnal travelers attempted to cross the ford without payment; the frogs were the "lock" to the community's revenue. The name is alternatively ascribed to a local swamp, long drained, known as Frog Loch. The frog-lock icon is emblazoned on both the city seal and the Farina coat of arms; chocolate versions may be purchased at every local confectionery. The city has numerous significant buildings, including the Hall of Taxes, which features fortified windows and a crenelated roofline; the equally imposing Debtors' Prison; and the Ducal Armory, with its wide parade ground and attached Museum of Uniforms and Flags. When Edwig of Farina, then only a baron, married the Countess of Paindecampagne, he sought to mark his newly elevated rank by renaming Froglock with the seemingly more prestigious if meaningless homophone of Phraugheloch. The local populace, in a rare display of subversion, refused to comply, and after several years of escalating penalties and increasingly brazen acts of sabotage, Edwig relented. Today Phraugheloch refers only to the ducal palace, a neoclassical structure of singular dimension and finish even by the criteria of the city in which it stands.

A Missive From ~Tips~
~~The Booted Maestro~~

Dear Trudy,

We are ~~coming home~~ returning to the Empire of Lax! Finally!
The sultans wedding is over at last—I didnt know it took so
many weeks + so many festivities just to get married—I am so
tired! It will be nice to be back where there are clouds + rain +
actual cold. I can barely remember what cold feels like.

I know you keep asking when you will see me + believe me I
want to see you ~~just as~~ very much but Felis doesnt think its wise
for me to return to Bacio given what Hans keeps ~~threatening~~
saying. Even though ~~he~~ Hans signed a contract with Felis, if I
returned he could still make me stay + work at the mill. Felis
gets so ~~furious~~ angry that Id be _wasted_ like that—I dont know
if Id be wasted but I surely wouldnt enjoy ~~working~~ milling the
way I enjoy this. Felis got us new uniforms—I wish I could show
you. I ~~know~~ think you would like them but I can just imagine
what Hans would say!

I think about you every day + I hope you like these earrings
they cost me ~~two months wages~~ a bit of money but dont worry,
I dont have anyone to spend on but you. I have no one I _want_

to spend on but you. I bet theyll be so ~~beuti~~ beautiful with
your hair! Red + green ~~harmen~~ harmonize because theyre opposites—thats what Felis says + while I dont understand how
colors can be opposites or how harmony works even in music
let alone hair, I think hes right about this one. I wish I could
see you wearing them. I will someday, I promise. ~~You are I will
always~~ Affectionately—

— Tips

A Life Unforeseen

The Story of Fortitude of Bacio, Commonly Known as Trudy, as Told to Her Daughter

Privately Printed and Circulated

RUDY COULD HARDLY shut her eyes that night, she was so exhausted and worried and—for goodness' sake, they had a queen at the Duke's Arms! A *queen!* Sleeping in the second-best room!

Which, Trudy could not help but note with a satisfied nod, was precisely how a queen should act, giving the best room to her suffering ladies-in-waiting. Truly, as Trudy pondered it, this old woman did everything as a queen should. She didn't even call herself queen! Her traveling companions—those fit enough to speak, anyway—called her Nonna Ben, an insolence that had stunned Trudy when first she heard it. To think that the queen of a country—or in this case the queen mother—enjoyed the same endearment as Bacio grannies, with that commonplace "Ben" tacked on the end . . . remarkable. The queen had scurried for hours about the inn just like a grannie too, verifying that every member of her entourage was comfortable. Trudy hoped she herself would always be as solicitous, particularly (should such an anomaly ever come to pass) to those beneath her.

Princess Wisdom, on the other hand, was . . . different. The featherbrained farm girls had described her as graceful and lovely and the best princess they'd ever met—which wasn't saying much given their life experience. They found it astonishing that a young woman of royal blood would enjoy currying manes and polishing harnesses. Hurrying across the courtyard, Trudy at last caught a glimpse of this celebrity laughing with the grooms as though they'd been friends all their lives. Trudy's reaction, however, wasn't amusement or awe or even dismay: it was horror. Misery flooded her so violently that she clawed at her throat for breath. It was her own misery that she saw, looking at the princess. Her own future unhappiness.

She fled the stable yard at once. However charming the princess might appear to others, Trudy wanted nothing to do with her.

So that night, while preparing the second-best room for sleep, Trudy deflected the suggestion that she join the Montagne contingent, much as it hurt to disappoint the queen. Simply standing near the princess—who by the way appeared quite unaware of Trudy's existence—made Trudy quake. She excused herself quick as she could and kept busy with countless other crucial tasks until she fell into bed.

No, she could not go galavanting off with these foreigners, no matter how much she enjoyed dear Nonna Ben, how desperately they required assistance, or how pleasant it was (when she permitted herself such vanity) to imagine herself a lady-in-waiting. She needed to stay as far from Princess Wisdom as possible; her sight made that fact abundantly clear. Besides, the Duke's Arms needed her too. Eds needed her, however infrequently he expressed his gratitude. Most of all, Tips needed her. She'd made a promise to wait for him, and wait she would: in Bacio. In two years' time he'd finish his apprenticeship and return to her. And if by some miracle he finished early, she would be here for him, as she'd vowed. Comforted beyond measure by the certainty of this logic, and by the peace of mind that came from knowing she would never, ever in her life eat an oyster, she drifted off to sleep.

✿ ✿ ✿

The next morning, Trudy awoke before dawn. There was so much to do! Could she possibly turn six-month-old pumpkins into a dish fit for royalty—or at the very least a dish fit for breakfast? And the second-best tablecloths (the best had been used at dinner)—what if the mice had gotten into them? She hadn't thought to check! What about the lunch roasts, broth for the invalids, flowers for the tables . . .

Trudy was pondering pudding recipes with the cook and attempting to get some labor out of the featherbrains—had none of these girls ever folded a napkin?—when the mail rider arrived from Froglock. Normally Trudy would drop every task, but today she was far too busy even to pay the man notice. He, however, sought her out especially and extracted from his great-coat a soiled, much-stamped package no larger than his cupped palm—a package from Tips!

Almost quivering in frustration, Trudy diligently verified that the cook understood the task before her and that the feath-erbrains weren't making too great a hash of the linens before she slipped outside for a moment of peace.

She ducked into the laundry shed. No one would dare fol-low her there—they might get put to work! But laundry had not yet begun that morn, and Trudy, alone at last, studied the small package tied with string, neatly knotted (oh, Tips), and addressed in his schoolboy hand.

Using the wee scissors she carried always for a thousand different emergencies, Trudy cut the string and drew open the paper. Nestled inside, like an egg in a nest, was a dark wooden box carved with leaves and berries. What a lovely, lovely gift! Trudy cradled it tenderly, and it took her some time to realize that the box had a hinge and clasp.

Slowly. she lifted the lid. Rich velvet of the deepest blue lined the inside, cupping the most beautiful earrings Trudy had ever seen. Had ever even imagined. Fine-spun gold, so delicate it could be the work of fairies, clasped two tear-dropped jade stones. Trudy held one to a sunbeam to study it more clearly, then exclaimed as the polished facets captured the light, glow-ing with the brilliant, depthless green of life, and spring.

The stones were not jade. They were—they had to be—emeralds.

Overcome, she crumpled down on a bucket. The bucket, luckily, was inverted, though she probably wouldn't have noticed if she'd ended up hip deep in suds. What girl in Bacio—in all of Alpsburg—had ever been so privileged? Emerald earrings! She would save them—hide them away where no one could ever find them!—and wear them for Tips's return.

Tucking the earrings back into their elegant little case, Trudy noticed at last the scrap of notepaper folded beneath the velvet: he was returning! Not to Bacio, to be sure (though simply thinking these words set Trudy's heart beating), but at least to the empire. Oh, to know he would be that much closer.

If only Hans and Jens weren't so absolutely horrid! Tips had every right to fear being seized; his brothers were lazy and stupid and utterly unsuited to someone as wonderful as he. No wonder Tips never wrote them; it was bad enough that Trudy had to pass along his gifts, which they treated *so* rudely, and her as well . . . At least this time Tips wasted no words on them. Trudy had enough responsibility today without a trip to the mill.

She should return to work; she'd squandered too much time already. But she lingered a moment more. Blushing at her immodesty, she released a curl of hair from her kerchief and held it beside the gem. Red and green did go together; she'd heard this before. But her hair, with emeralds? It was hard to tell. If Tips said it, though, then it must be true. Tips knew everything.

Tucking the letter and box into a deep pocket, and her hair beneath its cloth, she hurried back to the inn.

The disorder she had left not ten minutes earlier was now thrice as loud, the small kitchen seething with people . . . Trudy elbowed her way through the crowd, angry now at those silly, stupid farm girls. What had they done, on today of all days, to cause such a ruckus?

The commotion did not center, however, on the feather-brains, who stood to one side with gaping mouths, but—Trudy would never have believed it were she not observing it with her own eyes—on Princess Wisdom and old Nonna Ben, yet in their dressing gowns, looming over the mail rider, who sat huddled on a stool like a snared truant.

"Tell me!" The princess shook the man. "Where is he *exactly,* and when did he get there? Speak, man!"

The mail rider stuttered, overwhelmed by this onslaught.

Trudy's eyes met the queen's, and in that instant she knew what the mail rider had told them, what the queen would ask of her, and what—inevitably—her answer would be.

The Gentle Reflections
of Her Most Noble Grace,
Wilhelmina, Duchess of Farina,
within the Magnificent Phraugheloch Palace
in the City of Froglock

Well! My frail nerves cannot—simply cannot—survive such trauma!—I would collapse were it not abundantly clear that without my firm hand this duchy would dissolve into chaos.

The emperor—Rüdiger IV himself!—has appeared at the gates of Froglock with his entire ridiculous menagerie!—which Farina is expected to feed!

Tigers and elephants—and soldiers!—and accountants! And we're to feed them!

All those prying men with their prying questions—as though the wealth moving through my duchy belongs to anyone but myself!

I am of course already on tenterhooks awaiting Roger's betrothed—who has still not arrived—she cares not a whit for the lengths to which I have gone to prepare Phraugheloch for royalty.

Poor Handsome is so overcome that he was finally provoked into a small nip—and while the surgeons assure me they can reattach the boy's finger, my son had the nerve to demand that my poor little dog be locked up!—and furthermore claimed that he had been inspired to this insolence by the thought of Princess Wisdom!

It is a woman's duty not to inspire a man but to submit to him, and a man's duty to command his wife—a dictum which I was forever commanding of my late husband, and which he was utterly incapable of enforcing—I will not see that Montagne minx dominate my son so!

That the Kingdom of Montagne lords itself over the Duchy of Farina—though we have ten times the land and peoples —burns me like a brand.

I will have that throne.

THE IMPERIAL ENCYCLOPEDIA OF LAX

8TH EDITION

Printed in the Capital City of Rigorus
by Hazelnut & Filbert, Publishers to the Crown

RÜDIGER IV

The rule of Rüdiger IV, the Spindle Kaiser, culminated the struggle between the Empire of Lax and its most powerful domains. The grandson of Wilhelm VIII on his mother's side, Rüdiger had no aspirations to the throne and was declared heir only after Wilhelm's sons—the Three Disappointers, as they were subsequently known—fathered nineteen girls. Rüdiger took the throne at age thirty-two and ruled for fifty-eight years. While maintaining a permanent campaign on the northern frontier and leading his empire in multiple wars, Rüdiger made significant advances in diplomacy. He formalized relations with the Sultanate of Ahmb, surveyed Lax's eastern boundary, and negotiated with his many subject states to reduce the tolls that jeopardized imperial trade. The widespread popularity of the names Roger, Ruggiero, Rutger, Hrothgar, Rogelio, Rufiger, and similar derivates of Rüdiger speaks to the nobility's efforts to curry favor within the imperial court and should in no way be considered a demonstration of affection. In his later years, Rüdiger IV traveled throughout the empire and beyond with his private circus and military escort. It is not unthinkable that this "Circus Primus" may have served as a façade for covert proceedings, as the emperor and his troupe were present for the Feldspar Assumption, the Mar y Muntanya Border Crusade, and the Fourth Altercation of Scampi; Rüdiger's role in Wisdom's Kiss, much parsed by scholars, exemplifies the tumult that often shadowed the Circus Primus ensemble. Perhaps not surprisingly, his later reign was tainted by charges of irresponsibility, even senility, accusations that Rüdiger did not or could not dispute, and his legacy does not adequately reflect his earlier achievements.

A Life Unforeseen

The Story of Fortitude of Bacio, Commonly Known as Trudy, as Told to Her Daughter

Privately Printed and Circulated

O THINK! For so many years Trudy had burned to reunite with Tips, and now it was about to happen. And not sitting in lonesome Bacio twiddling her thumbs, but by traveling to Froglock—where Tips was this very minute, guarding the emperor with the other soldiers!—and she was traveling in a *coach,* with a *queen,* as (Trudy could pinch herself!) a veritable *lady-in-waiting!*

Although Trudy didn't need a pinch: pain came easily enough simply by glancing at the young woman who sat across from her scowling out the window. Every time she looked at Princess Wisdom, Trudy shuddered. Fortunately the princess did not seem to notice. In fact, she did not acknowledge Trudy's presence at all, and rarely spoke. This, Trudy comforted herself, must have been what her sight had warned her of: an inexplicable royal snubbing. If so, Trudy would tolerate it with dignity, and instead focus her attention, happily, on the queen.

All her life Trudy had longed for a grandmother. Not the fairy version found in stories, but a real old lady who would praise and treasure her. At last she had chanced upon this marvelous species of human, and while Nonna Ben, to be sure, was not *her* grandmother, nonetheless she rejoiced in the woman's presence as a sunflower, turning its head to follow the path of the sun across the sky, absorbs every warming ray.

Trudy was supremely fortunate (so Nonna Ben informed her) to have learned to sew, for she now had the unenviable task, within this rocking carriage ere it drew to a halt at the imposing front doors of Phraughloch Palace, of fitting herself in one of Lady Modesty's gowns, the blue silk so lovely that Trudy winced to pierce the fabric, no matter how Nonna Ben chuckled, and repeated that her beautiful stitching would only improve it.

As Trudy wielded her needle in and out, in and out, they chatted about the myriad arcane duties of a lady-in-waiting. Oh, it was so complicated! For example, one addressed a queen or king as *Your Majesty*—everyone knew *that*—but a princess or prince was only *Your Highness,* sometimes with *Royal* tucked in halfway through. The emperor garnered *Your Imperial Majesty,* counts and barons *Lord* or *Lady,* and dukes such as Farina's Duke Roger *Your Grace,* though Roger's mother insisted on *Most Noble Grace,* which for some reason set Nonna Ben and even Wisdom to giggling whenever they uttered it. Easy for them to laugh; they already knew the rules, and doubtless had behaved perfectly all their lives.

"Don't fret." Ben patted Trudy. "I know you'll instinctively do it right . . . Let's try this on, shall we?" She helped Trudy out of her simple homespun and slipped the gown, pins yet in it, over her head. "Child, you should be a seamstress . . . It fits to perfection."

Trudy's blush scorched her face. "But it's—begging your pardon—it's too low."

Ben, turning Trudy this way and that in the swaying coach, laughed out loud. "I should say not! The ducal court will be so busy admiring your décolletage that they shan't notice you're the entirety of our staff. Doesn't she look grand, Dizzy? Granddaughter?"

"It's fine," Wisdom answered, never taking her eyes from the wheat fields.

Nonna Ben shot Wisdom a very ungrandmotherly glare before helping Trudy out of the gown. "Thank goodness Lady Modesty is so portly; had we time enough, we could fashion the leftover material into a nice wrap. Or perhaps a set of curtains."

Trudy couldn't help smiling. Nonna Ben was so sweet to pretend she looked nice when it was clear she didn't—clear to Trudy, anyway, and obviously clear to the princess.

"That blue with your hair, and those earrings . . . are they a gift from a beau? I would say you're a lucky girl to have such a generous suitor, but really he's the lucky one, having a sweetheart as pretty as you."

Bent over her stitching, Trudy beamed to herself. Nonna Ben was wrong: it was she who was the lucky one—the luckiest girl in the world—to have a beau as wonderful and perfect as

Tips. It was almost as if Tips had sight himself, to send her these earrings so fortuitously. They did look lovely with the dress, and no one in Froglock would accuse her of putting on airs, for no one in Froglock knew her station . . . No one, that is, but Tips. They'd left Bacio so quickly that she'd barely had time to scribble a note for the next mail rider—a note Tips probably would not receive until after she'd arrived, not at the pace this carriage was moving. Never in her life had she traveled so fast, or so far—and to what a glorious destination!

Escoffier, asleep beside her, stretched his long black legs, and absently Trudy stroked the cat. Soon, soon, she'd see him. Soon she'd be with Tips again. Anticipation bubbled in her chest like a fountain.

THE IMPERIAL ENCYCLOPEDIA
OF LAX

8TH EDITION

Printed in the Capital City of Rigorus
by Hazelnut & Filbert, Publishers to the Crown

FORTITUDE OF BACIO

No birth record exists of Fortitude of Bacio, who was born soon after her mother's arrival in Alpsburg; the woman perished of infective fever ten years later. Fortitude remained in Bacio until Year 28 of the reign of Rüdiger IV, when a royal party traveling from Montagne halted there after the entourage was decimated by food poisoning, an event immortalized in the comic ballad "Pass the Bucket, Queenie!" Desperate for assistance en route to the wedding of her granddaughter to the Duke of Farina, and apparently unaware of the girl's supposed foresight, the queen mother of Montagne offered Fortitude a position as lady-in-waiting. In agreeing to serve attendance—a responsibility for which the girl had no training whatsoever beyond a childhood spent as a kitchen wench, and certainly no breeding—Fortitude of Bacio unwittingly tendered herself as yet another catalyst in the great turbulence about to reshape the Empire of Lax. Controversy continues to surround the girl's preternatural abilities, fanned by recent analysis (see, for example, *The Imperial Gastric and Psychiatric Journal of Ajar,* v. 84ff). Regardless, the arrival of Fortitude in the city of Froglock, along with Emperor Rüdiger IV, Princess Wisdom of Montagne, and the young swordsman Tomas Müller with his impresario Felis el Gato, would play a critical role in the forthcoming upheaval of Wisdom's Kiss, and it may be stated without exaggeration that her presence determined the life and death of two nations.

PART II

PHRAUGHELOCH,
SEAT OF INFAMY

THE SUPREMELY PRIVATE DIARY
OF ~~WISDOM~~ *Dizzy* ˅ OF MONTAGNE

Any Soul Who Contemplates Even Glancing

at the Pages of this Volume Will

~~*Be Transformed into a Toad*~~

Suffer a Most Excruciating Punishment.

On This You Have My Word.

Thursday—evening—

We are within an hour of Froglock—would that we arrived this v. second as I am fiercely weary of this ghastly carriage! I have been imprisoned within this lurching monster for all the afternoon as Nonna says 'twould be unseemly if I trotted beside or heaven forbid rode atop with that wonderful coachman—'tis true I probably could not keep pace with the horses—not in skirts anyway—but to be trapped within this dusty upholstery when the sky for once is blue & the clouds so crisp I could ride them . . . I am a victim pure & simple. A sacrifice to protocol.

Nonna & that serving girl have become the best of friends—it is horrible to behold. Nonna praises her incessantly—her figure—her stitches—her respect for decorum—each time pointing out my shortcomings with words or tone. It is not my fault I have no bosom! I would rather pad my dresses than squeeze myself in as Mrs. Sprat must! And then T was so good—so diligent—to spend the day altering Mrs. Sprat's gown—I would have been rendered sick from the motion of the carriage but she did not seem affected & she does have a v. lovely stitch—if I could sew half so well I'd have saved myself a lifetime of scoldings. Nonna kept droning on about how terribly she herself used to sew but I know she is referring to me.

We have just departed our fourth inn of the day where we stopped yet again for fresh horses & to change as we cannot appear at P in our traveling clothes!—& T was so helpful dressing Nonna in her green velvet or so Nonna stated at least five & twenty times. As we have suffered the loss of our hair-dresser I was forced to don a wig—by good fortune Nonna remembered to pack it!—& so I now sit with stays & horsehair poking me in countless places—I cannot wait to relieve this discomfort—but worse than this is T! That blue gown made Mrs. Sprat look like a breaching whale but "Lady Fortitude" (which is what we must call her & it does sound v. impressive however much T squirms when we speak it) has stitched it into a marvel—clearly she wishes the bodice more discreet tho I thought serving maids aspired to lusty proportions—& most ladies I know would renounce their titles for such an aspect!

Nonna insisted T remove her headscarf—the girl is so irritatingly diffident!—& with thirty seconds' effort & four combs piled that hair into the most glorious pompadour I have ever seen. With natural ringlets! I could not help sighing in envy though my praise only irked her. She now sits frowning out the coach window—completely ungrateful for her blessings. I would be the happiest of girls if I were she.

O! I am to see Roger! I had forgotten completely! It has been so many months that I fear—on top of all my other worries! —that I will not recognize him! How awful that would be. How v. awful indeed.

From the Desk

of the

Queen Mother of Montagne,

& Her Cat

My Dearest Temperance, Queen of Montagne:

Granddaughter, forgive this rough hand, but a trotting carriage does not provide the smoothest of venues in which to write. Yet I cannot delay in conveying my delight at your good fortune — which I now know, thanks to the devotion and resolve of the imperial mail service! 'Twas most remarkable — even your sister, who has been in a rare sulk the entire day, brightened at the experience. The westerly mail rider, having been informed of our proximity by the keeper of the inn we had only recently departed, raced to intercept us that he might tender the queen mother of Montagne correspondence from the queen. Handing me your missive with a flourish, he then continued on his journey to Froglock.

Teddy darling, such marvelous news! To think you have a suitor! Do you not fear you shall reduce your dear Nonna Ben to apoplexy by leaving me in suspense? Who is this young man you love like no other? I must have more detail! If the match proves as felicitous as you describe, it will, I confess, offer me much relief. Not only will you have found happiness, but the threat to Montagne will thus be greatly diminished. While it is grand to see Farina bound to a junior member of the Montagne family, particularly one (as well you know!) so clearly resistant to domination, yet I still fear Wilhelmina. The sooner you are wedded, the safer Montagne will be! Not — I assure you — that this is reason alone to marry; not nearly. But do enjoy your courtship, for it is a delight beyond measure to feel cherished.

Within our conveyance, on the other hand, emotions drift far indeed from love — and rather close to irritation and pique. While my satisfaction with young Trudy swells by the hour, for some reason your sister dislikes her. I cannot imagine why, as the girl is fetching and mindful and has the loveliest tresses, although I confess she expresses little enthusiasm for Dizzy as well. It was like riding today with two feuding she-cats; Escoffier was wise to sleep through it — and you to avoid it altogether!

I must say that for all Trudy's assistance and her skill with a needle, the girl continues to puzzle. At lunch she inexplicably leapt up, serviette in hand, a moment before the tavern keeper spilt a pitcher of water. It was as if she sensed the crisis — promptly averted thanks to her — ere it transpired. She knew, too, both times I intended to ask that she accompany us — last night when she demurred, and again this morning when she acceded ere the first word had crossed my lips. I cannot help but suspect some sort of magic — ironic indeed after our vow!

The possibility intrigued me enough to pry rather indiscreetly into her background, though I made sure to do so while Dizzy was elsewhere (she has forged quite a fellowship with our coachman, and believes me ignorant of their contests in spitting). But Trudy, it seems, has no background, or rather knows nothing of it. Her mother arrived in Bacio enceinte, never spoke of her origins or of the girl's father, and was taken by fever some years ago. It is a tender subject for her — as it would be for any of us — and I did not pursue it. Moreover, although Trudy carries the charming appellation of <u>Fortitude,</u> her mother's name was <u>Mina,</u> which is no virtue with which I am familiar — the family most definitely did not hail from Montagne! Altogether most peculiar, though I am delighted to have for once an attendant who anticipates spills rather than causing them.

Behold, we approach the city of Froglock and our first skirmish with Wilhelmina. I am certain that Montagne is thriving in your hands, and look forward to the conclusion of all this excitement that I might return to my kingdom and meet your charming suitor for myself! In the meantime, however, I do wish that one could outfit old women with armor. I should feel much safer in Wilhelmina's presence enclosed in steel.

Your resolute grandmother, all atremble,
Ben

THE IMPERIAL ENCYCLOPEDIA OF LAX

8TH EDITION

Printed in the Capital City of Rigorus
by Hazelnut & Filbert, Publishers to the Crown

WILHELMINA THE ILL-TEMPERED

Born to minor nobility in central Lax, Wilhelmina rose to a position of unrivaled prominence within her generation. Her father, Edwig, Baron of Farina, from a young age proved adept at the intrigues of court life, marrying himself to the far more eminent Countess of Paindecampagne; Wilhelmina, named in honor of Emperor Wilhelm VIII, was betrothed to the Duke of Höchsteland while still a child. Thus the family in only two generations climbed from the lowest to the highest of noble ranks, and obscure Farina swelled into a vast and powerful duchy. Wilhelmina was left sole ruler when her husband, and then their eldest son, Ruttger, died in service to the imperial crown. Through her insistence, the family received as compensation the Duchy of Sottocenere and the city of Bridgeriver, increasing Wilhelmina's wealth considerably. Feared and admired for her ambition and shrewdness, she served as regent until Roger, the middle son, attained his majority; her subsequent designation of dowager was universally considered a screen to her true authority. Now in possession of lands and tributaries surrounding Montagne on four sides, Wilhelmina announced that the tiny kingdom and its title would be absorbed, willingly or otherwise, by Farina. When her diplomatic overtures were rejected by Providence and Benevolence, the queen and queen mother of Montagne, the duchess began assembling a sizable army at the kingdom's borders. Following the death of Providence, Wilhelmina shifted her strategy to merging the two states through the marriage of Roger to Montagne's new queen, Temperance. These negotiations proved ineffective when Roger instead selected Temperance's younger sister, Wisdom, for his bride. Initially enraged by her son's choice, Wilhelmina later insisted the wedding take place in the city of Froglock and extended all her support to the nuptial preparations . . .

A Life Unforeseen

The Story of Fortitude of Bacio, Commonly Known as Trudy, as Told to Her Daughter

Privately Printed and Circulated

RUDY GAPED out the carriage window at Froglock: more people, more buildings—and more soldiers! —than she had seen in her entire life! How could people live so crowded together, like . . . like bees in a hive? And, most important, how would she ever locate Tips?

The princess and Nonna Ben, packing up their papers and fussing with their gowns, paid Trudy no heed, though Ben did glance out at an avenue draped in the imperial colors, each banner paired—every dimension and detail matched—with Farina's flag and coat of arms. The old woman smiled. "Thank heavens that the emperor himself is in Froglock . . . Now she has someone else to tie her gloves in a knot about."

Trudy had spent hours enough in the carriage to know who *she* was, and no longer to goggle at any mention of Rüdiger IV. To think: only one day ago she had been tending wayward hens, and now she was *Lady Fortitude.* Once more she touched her earrings. Perhaps, she thought hopefully, the emeralds would keep people from staring at her hair—not to mention the expanse of skin between her chin and the lacy top of her gown. She had never in her life dressed so! Were she in need of lavish tips, such exposure might be appropriate, but Trudy preferred penniless modesty . . . Yet again she blushed, though this time at least she did not look down. *You'll only draw attention,* Ben had kept warning her, as Princess Wisdom glowered.

Much as it hurt to look at Wisdom, Trudy could not resist another glance in her direction. The princess's restrained gown emphasized her slender beauty, and with the wig—so perfect, so *fitting,* thought Trudy—she resembled nothing so much as a china figurine, though one alive with verve and wit and incontestable authority. Even motionless and scowling, standing without effort in the swaying carriage, the princess glowed.

Is it possible to fear and admire simultaneously? Trudy wondered. She would ask Tips. Soon—oh, blissfully soon!—she would see Tips, and ask him.

Escorted by the ducal men-at-arms, the carriage passed through another magnificent gate, into a courtyard crowded with glittering courtiers.

Nonna Ben chuckled. "I wondered how our arrival would be handled . . ."

Just for a moment, Trudy saw fear cross Wisdom's face. Then the princess composed herself into an inscrutable regal mask. She looked over Trudy's shoulder. "That's Roger in purple, on the left."

Of course that's the duke! Trudy thought. Even *I* know that! She really must think I'm dim.

The carriage slowed to a halt. Trudy touched the beaded reticule hanging from her wrist: handkerchief—eau de toilette —fan—extra gloves . . . So much responsibility! Not that the princess needed anything—nor doubtless would ever ask *her*—but Trudy intended to do her best. If the duty of a lady-in-waiting was to tender her lady assistance "before she even knows she needs it," then Trudy was probably more competent than most—or so she hoped.

The carriage door swung open. Ben exited, then Wisdom. Trudy found herself stepping down, a wigged footman at each elbow, as she struggled to remember if she should thank them.

No one—such a relief!—paid her the slightest attention. All eyes were on Nonna Ben, Princess Wisdom, and an older woman who cradled a lap dog and without moving her head managed to convey that she was looking down her nose at the newcomers: Duchess Wilhelmina. The entire court, it appeared, was arranged behind the duchess, gilded lanterns illuminating the jewels and gold of their ornaments. Roger beamed at his betrothed.

"Your Majesty. Your Highness." The duchess uttered this without emotion, though several listeners—queen and princess included—stiffened.

"Your *Royal* Highness," Roger interjected quickly, stepping forward. He bowed to Nonna Ben and kissed her hand. He kissed Wisdom's and beamed even wider.

Ben dropped her head, ever so slightly, toward Roger. "Your Grace—Your Most Noble Grace—may I proffer our heartfelt apologies for this catastrophe of a journey. I beg forgiveness and pray you take no insult from it, for 'twas the elements and the gods, not ill intent, that delayed us so."

The queen mother's words hung in the air. The crowd—or so Trudy sensed; certainly *she* held her breath—waited to observe how the duchess would react to such eloquent and earnest regret.

The silence was shattered, most abruptly, by Wilhelmina's terrier, who barked and squirmed for release, glaring behind Trudy. Turning with the others to ascertain the basis of this canine fury, Trudy observed Escoffier leisurely descending the carriage steps, his tail in the air.

"Think nothing of it," said the duchess, responding at last to Nonna Ben. "We would that you—valued safety—over speed"—here struggling to maintain her grip on the dog.

Tail swaying, Escoffier strolled to Ben's feet and sat. He licked one paw.

"How kind of you; your mercy speaks well of Farina, and the empire," Ben continued—her voice raised over the dog's hysterical barking, though her regal tone did not change.

The dog howled, and squirmed like a hooked fish, while Wilhelmina clung to his jeweled collar. Behind her, several members of her court were suddenly taken ill, or so it seemed from the coughing that broke out. Duke Roger—quite handsome, Trudy thought; even statelier than his representation—stroked his mustache repeatedly, and with unusual force.

Oh, Trudy realized at last, they're not sick: they're simply trying not to laugh! From the corner of her eye, Trudy could see Wisdom clenching her jaw, and the knuckles of the princess's fists were so white that her fingernails must have sliced her palms. Yet she otherwise remained serene—inordinately serene—and neither queen nor duchess, in voice or visage, gave the slightest acknowledgment of the great charade taking place between them.

"When word came of your approach, Your Majesty," Wilhelmina explained loudly, over the barking, "We were en route to the circus grounds to enjoy a performance by His Imperial Majesty's private troupe. We beg you join us . . ." The terrier twisted in her hands.

Escoffier took this opportunity to yawn—the longest yawn Trudy had ever observed. His pink tongue curled and his white teeth gleamed, and just for a moment, as his jaws closed, he looked straight into the eyes of the dog.

At once the yapping trebled in volume.

Ben smiled serenely. "That would be lovely." She turned to Trudy. "Lady Fortitude, perhaps you might attend to our trunks? It has been such a long journey—"

At last the terrier, losing control completely, bit Duchess Wilhelmina. She dropped it with a hiss. At the same instant, Escoffier leapt into Trudy's arms.

"Also, see that the cat's fed, will you?" With that, the queen swept her gown away from the lunging dog and took Roger's elbow. "I did not know you had *circus grounds,* Your Grace," she murmured, sounding perhaps too sincere. "I am quite curious to observe them . . ."

Quickly a nobleman stepped up to escort Wisdom, who engaged the man in a conversation on their travels, which, she assured him, had passed without incident.

Rubbing her wrist, Wilhelmina sent her pet a dagger-eyed glare before stomping to the front of the procession, the glittering crowd behind her. Several footmen circled the little dog, none too keen to approach, and when Trudy tried to nudge the dog away from her precious skirts, it snapped at her ankle.

Escoffier adjusted his position in Trudy's arms and blinked at her. Trudy was quite convinced that had he been human, he would have been laughing.

Memoirs
of the
Master Swordsman
FELIS EL GATO

Impresario Extraordinaire ✦ Soldier of Fortune
Mercenary of Stage & Empire

LORD OF THE LEGENDARY
FIST OF GOD
Famed Throughout the Courts and Countries of the World
&
The Great Sultanate
✳ THE BOOTED MAESTRO ✳

Written in His Own Hand~All Truths Verified~
All Boasts Real

A Most Marvelous Entertainment,
Not to Be Missed!

☞

I MUST HERE RELAY a singular incident that transpired whilst we domiciled in Froglock. Unfortunately the vast responsibilities of my position—for by this point I was nothing less than *second in command*, which Emperor Rüdiger IV himself called me, in the presence of bystanders—did not allow me to observe this event directly. The repeated recountings by others, however, over many weeks subsequent, permit me to relay the tale within these pages.

From the moment of our entry into Froglock, we had heard talk of Wisdom of Montagne, the princess betrothed to the Duke of Farina, whose arrival had been much delayed; rumors swirled that the royal delegation had been sickened en route. At last they were sighted, and when their carriage that dusk passed through the gates of the palace of Phraugheloch, 'twas a dusty and mediocre showing it made.

Anticipating their entrance, Dowager Duchess Wilhelmina assembled a welcoming party in the palace courtyard. I myself could never speak ill of such a noble and handsome woman and have sought to defend her from various slanders, such as how she kept her youngest son in military service in hopes that his death would gain her more land, which is a vicious falsehood I would never under pain of torture repeat. Froglock's more critical citizens similarly whispered that in orchestrating this public greeting, Wilhelmina sought to put Montagne's dishevelment—inevitable after a journey of such length, and so ill-fortuned—to her own advantage. Moreover, in greeting the queen mother while standing, the duchess would circumvent the convention of offering one's seat to royalty, a point of protocol which the woman—or so her unsympathetic subjects implied—particularly resented.

The carriage came to a rest, and the two Montagne royals and their lady-in-waiting exited its confines—again, I only quote the witnesses there present—in remarkably good form given the stress of many days' travel and the speed with which they had hurried. The usual pleasantries commenced but were interrupted almost at once when a sable-haired cat emerged from the coach to join his mistress, the queen mother. The duchess as it transpired was holding her own small terrier, which promptly and in the inevitable manner of its breed attempted, with much vocalizing, to leave her grip and pursue the feline.

The duchess—here again I only repeat others' reports and in no way seek to impugn the nobility of Her Most Noble Grace—was thus presented with a dilemma of no small significance. Were she to acknowledge the misbehavior of the creature sounding in her arms, she would be forced in the most literal manner to *retreat* before her rival in order to remove the offending creature. Therefore she ignored the disturbance, which increased by the moment as the cat, via an escalating series of provocations that appeared to be almost intentional, drove the dog to near madness. Only a corpse could have been expected to maintain composure in the face of such hilarity, and while no member of the duchess's retinue lost complete control, it would be many hours before the last of them was fit for presentation, and a month at least before the dog—a great favorite of the duchess's, sadly—could appear in public without upsetting the solemn equilibrium of the court.

The queen mother and princess of Montagne, on the other hand, emerged from this skirmish unscathed (as, I might note, did the cat). Intimations of witchcraft had shadowed

Benevolence of Montagne since her girlhood, and though I myself would never heed such denigrations, the uncanny and artfully timed behavior of the black cat did nothing to still the tongues of those gullible or instigative enough to fuel such hearsay. Yet even those of us too wise to swallow tales of sorcery recognized that the queen departed the scene of battle as the unquestioned victrix.

THE IMPERIAL ENCYCLOPEDIA OF LAX

8TH EDITION

Printed in the Capital City of Rigorus
by Hazelnut & Filbert, Publishers to the Crown

CIRCUS PRIMUS

Of all the achievements of Emperor Rüdiger IV, none was so memorable as Circus Primus. A lifelong passion for this entertainment led Rüdiger while still a lad to found a small circus for the entertainment of the imperial staff. In time he developed this private pleasure into a tool of statehood, challenging various fiefs and federation members to outdo each other within the ring. Controversies that in other reigns would have escalated to warfare now resolved themselves without bloodshed, though concussions and fractures were admittedly rife, and even the most recalcitrant of his vassals found themselves forced to accommodate and provision the ensemble. Circus Primus hosted myriad notable artists, including Raphael the Dancing Otter, the Flying Garbanzo Brothers, and the Elephantine Stiltdancers. Without question, however, the best-remembered performance remains the Globe d'Or, gifted to the emperor by the Sultan of Ahmb.

This metallic hot-air balloon—allegedly gold, and ensorcelled—promptly became the centerpiece of the circus and proved so popular that the emperor would credit its powers of diversion in the suppression of two rebellions. In addition to the requisite basket that the balloon hoisted midair, the Globe d'Or served as platform for acrobats such as the Master of Air, a skydiver of peerless artistry, and the Blind Men of Mince juggling act. It was said that the emperor loved Globe d'Or more than his five sons, as they together could not lift him as high as did this marvelous balloon. Following the emperor's death, Circus Primus disbanded, many of its employees finding continued fame with other troupes or in other livelihoods.

A MISSIVE FROM TIPS ~~THE BOOTED MAESTRO~~

Dear Trudy,

We are ~~home~~ in Farina — in the city of Froglock! I almost cried when I saw puddles again, I was so happy — the desert is ~~much too awful~~ not for me! Its nice to know youre only one days very long horse ride away — ~~You know that~~ I hope you know I would visit if I could, but its just too dangerous. Besides I have no time, we are working day + night without rest.

Yesterday we were crossing the Daft Bridge into Froglock — we have a very long ~~proccession~~ ~~parede~~ parade as the circus grows with every place we visit! — + the river was so high + fearsome because of the flooding, + one of the camel mares (we have camels too now, another gift from the sultan) panicked + started pounding down the bridge knocking people left + right — camels are very tall + very fast so you can imagine how frightful it was, ~~partickul~~ particularly with everyone screaming. Luckily I was ~~walking~~ marching some ways ahead + could see her coming, + before I really had time to think I was standing on the bridge railing so I could jump on her, + as I was sailing thru the air I was thinking how much better this experience would be if you were ~~with me~~ here to see me safe! But I did manage to land on her more or less, + then climbed up her back which must be like climbing a sea serpent she was thrashing so much, + finally got her eyes covered—not easy at that speed!—+ luckily she calmed down. Poor Felis didnt know whether to scold me for _endangering my talents_ or praise me for _saving so many lives_—so he ~~comprimized~~ made do by simply patting me on the back + I was so covered in bruises I yelped! You wouldve laughed so hard if youd heard me.

Do you remember how you used to watch for Hans when we played by the mill? + how you cried when you first ~~set eyes on~~ saw Felis, but you said I had to go with him anyway? I still think about that, + how ~~signifikant~~ important that day was.

I will see you again someday I am sure, ~~I just dont know when~~ it might be years Im afraid before I make it back to Bacio. ~~I miss you I dont miss Bacio~~ I do not care for any of the ladies I meet as much as I care for you + how nice you have always been to me—

—Tips

A Life Unforeseen

The Story of Fortitude of Bacio, Commonly Known as Trudy, as Told to Her Daughter

Privately Printed and Circulated

RUDY UNPACKED as hastily as she could manage, desperate to go find Tips. To have this opportunity emerge—so fortuitously!—within minutes of her arrival in Froglock . . . She might never have such a possibility again.

Hasty, however, by no means meant slapdash, particularly given the complexity of the luggage, their accommodations, and the palace staff. As the maître du palais—a butler, Trudy gathered, not that she had any experience with such a profession—led her and Escoffier through the corridors in a parade of servants toting Montagne luggage, he explained the history and importance of the suite in which they were being installed, speaking to her as a peer, which—she realized belatedly—would be more than a little presumptuous if Trudy were in fact titled, and she was pleased to note that her blithe disregard for his familiarity greatly irked the man. Trudy's mother had always warned her that *ignorance never blesses a*

tongue, and Trudy now discovered the truth of this adage; the maître du palais misinterpreted her silence as clever feint, and his arrogance decayed into a fawning that increased with every passing minute.

Even if she had known what to say, however, Trudy would not have had energy to speak, so engrossed was she in the embellishments, garnishes, gildings, and objets d'art that mantled the palace's every surface. Draperies and paintings, carpets thick enough to hide a snake, chandeliers and candelabras, vases and flowers and great potted palms . . . What must these things have cost? And who was the poor soul assigned to dusting? How marvelous it would be to describe it to Tips! She smiled to herself (thus escalating the maître du palais's bluster) at the thought of Tips sending his letters to faraway Bacio—perhaps even now penning words she would not read for many days hence, until the real ladies-in-waiting, restored to health, made their way at last to Froglock and she could return to her gilt-free life in Alpsburg.

The actual task of unpacking proved easier than Trudy had anticipated, for three palace maids labored over the trunks, occasionally asking where Her Highness or Her Majesty wished an item. Trudy answered their queries to the best of her ability, reminding herself that Nonna Ben would graciously tolerate any mistakes and that Wisdom probably didn't care. She agreed that Her Majesty desired warm milk before retiring (Trudy would drink it if Nonna Ben didn't) and that Her Highness would want a bath at, oh, eight o'clock the next morning.

At last the maids finished—Trudy certain she would never locate a single item in that maze of rooms and wardrobes and chests of drawers—and withdrew. With a start she wondered if she should have tipped them. Certainly she would have expected recompense for such a service, but this was palace staff, not paid lodging, and besides she had no coins to offer.

There was so much, so very much, she did not know. Almost everything, in fact.

For example: could she walk through the palace confines unescorted? And if so, should she cover herself? Trudy certainly did not relish the thought of traipsing about with her hair and much of her chest exposed. Peering out the windows, she espied several women, and the fashion did seem inclined toward bare heads and décolletage. She sighed. At least she was spared the trouble of locating an appropriate wrap, for her old cloak (held with two fingers by the maid who unpacked it) had no place over such a gown, and she would never wear one of the queen's.

Checking to ensure Escoffier was safe—he had dismissively sniffed at a dish of chopped meat before curling up in the middle of a vast white bedspread—and that Tips's emeralds were still safe in her ears, Trudy departed the suite, copying as best she could the nonchalant confidence of the gentlewomen she had observed.

Within minutes, she was hopelessly lost, her sight completely unobliging. Where the guards were housed she had not a clue, she now realized, nor whether Tips would even be present.

Was there a separate location for imperial guards? If Tips was on duty—and given the descriptions of his long shifts, Trudy had no reason to suspect otherwise—would she be able to locate him? Would he even be able to speak to her? Perhaps he would not even recognize her! Now that she dwelled on the matter, Trudy was not sure she would recognize him—it had been six years, after all, since his departure from Bacio. Dark hair, brown eyes, long lashes, yes, but he was not a child anymore.

Yet she persevered, all too aware that the moment might never return. Descending every staircase she encountered, Trudy presently found herself in the cavernous kitchens, where the harried staff moved around her blue skirts as if Trudy were only ill-placed furniture. A life of toil had left the lass not entirely without resources, and her eyes alighted on a column of porters unloading vegetables. She trailed the empty-handed fellows down a passageway and presently found herself in a service courtyard where great wagons of foodstuffs rolled up and a fishmonger scraped ice from a pyramid of glassy-eyed mackerel.

On the theory that guards need horses and horses need roads, Trudy headed out the gate and soon enough caught sight of a phalanx of uniformed men. Acutely aware of her low neckline and conspicuous hair, Trudy, as she approached, braced herself for the men's leers. Yet the appraising eyes that greeted her arrival brimmed with admiration, not lechery.

"How might we help thee, fair lady?" asked one soldier.

"If any man speak ill of thee, but say the word and I shall have his hide," put in another.

"And I!" chimed several more.

Alas, it is experience and not foresight that makes wise men of us all. Trudy knew the soldiers wished to help—she saw that well enough—but she had no idea how, precisely, to ask. A lady didn't inquire after soldiers . . . Did she?

"Ah, yes . . . I'm looking for—someone *asked* me to look for—she wants to know—do you have a soldier named Tips? Or Tomas; Tomas Müller? . . ."

The men made a great show of concentration. "I must confess the name speaks not to me," the first soldier answered at last, with much regret.

"Oh. I am so sorry—he works for—he is with—the imperial guard—"

At this the man shifted. "Ah, the imperial guard . . . I know too well those swine."

His friends snickered. "Aye, and the flat of their swords!"

"Enough!" snapped the man. "If this fair lady seeks an imperial guard, her wish is my command. I shall escort her myself to their barracks!"

"And I!" interjected his companion, stepping possessively to Trudy's other side.

"Oh—thank you . . ." At least the men would bear her closer to her goal.

Which they did, one on each arm, and into Trudy's ears they poured a relentless assessment of their own fighting prowess, pausing in their grandiloquence only to belittle each other. It's like village boys with their wrestling, Trudy thought. So, knowing all too well the capacity and reasoning of village boys, through inquiries and flattery she played one off the other, thus deflecting attention from herself, until they reached a vast tented compound, bright with flaming torches, that could only belong to the emperor.

"We would speak to your man Tomas!" announced the first soldier to the entrance guard. "Tomas Miller!"

"Tomas *Müller,*" whispered Trudy, noting that her escort's bluster heightened an impression of internal quailing.

"No one here by that name," the guard replied. He turned to someone inside the gate. "Get the captain, will you?"

Trudy's escorts blanched, the first gulping audibly. Trudy blanched as well, for whatever was about to happen looked quite horrible to her sight.

All too soon a grizzled warrior appeared, sword and polishing cloth in hand. "You again . . . Here for another beating, or to bring me this wench in tribute?"

"I beg your pardon!" the first soldier exclaimed. "You have insulted grievously this fine lady, and as duke's representative I demand you—"

The captain sighed. "Shut it, will you? I've more important business—"

"You have insulted a lady!"

"Her? Lady?" The captain snorted. "Move on, all of you, before I smack you again."

The two soldiers flinched, but Trudy flinched still more. She could not tell what wounded her more: the imperial captain's dismissal—accurate, to be sure, but so humiliating!—or the deeper hurt at failing to locate Tips.

To their great credit, the duke's men escorted her back through the night to Phraugheloch Palace, though now without prattle. Trudy scarcely noticed. The man said *Tomas* wasn't there, but perhaps Tips still used his nickname. Or perhaps he didn't use Müller—given his brothers, it wouldn't be surprising . . . She should have used his master's name—what was it? Felix? No, Felis.

But she could not ask now. She couldn't ask *ever*. Not these soldiers, anyway, or that captain. And soon, too soon, she would return to Bacio . . . and might never see Tips again! Well, she'd see him someday, but not for years, and until that point she'd be all alone . . .

They arrived at last at an entrance, and Trudy, thanking the soldiers as best she could for their assistance, made her way with much stumbling and misdirection upstairs. Her weeping could no longer be restrained. Sopping at her nose—with Wisdom's handkerchief!—Trudy doddered down yet another corridor. They all looked alike. The passageways, the soldiers, the gentlewomen in their horrid fancy clothes . . . And nowhere, nowhere, Tips!

A servant girl passed, and Trudy turned away, reflexively shielding herself from prying eyes.

"This way, m'lady," the girl whispered, pointing to a door.

Mumbling thanks, Trudy let herself in—then ducked as a glass statuette shattered against a nearby wall.

"I will not listen!" Wisdom shouted at Ben, and hurled herself into the adjoining room, thunderously slamming the door behind her.

Ben stooped, creaking, to extract glass fragments from the carpet. She glanced at Trudy and sighed. "Welcome back, child."

From the Desk
of the
Queen Mother of Montagne,
& Her Cat

My Dearest Temperance, Queen of Montagne,

Granddaughter, what a night it has been. Our twilight arrival
at Phraugheloch (how long ago it seems!) must by now be
the talk of all the empire — I do think Escoffier is due a medal
for bravery in the face of an incensed duchess and her dog!
Much as I wanted to, I could not sing the cat's praises while
yet in the company of Wilhelmina, so instead I sent him to bed
and, feigning ignorance of our little duel of wits — or duel of
pets, I should say! — set off to observe at last Circus Primus.
To think the entire empire has had opportunity to see this
spectacular and we have not! — in my more equitable moments I comfort myself that Montagne has not behaved badly

enough to merit a visit — although given tonight's debacle, were I offered the option of going to my tomb rather than observing its charms, I would promptly choose eternal rest.

Allow me to elaborate . . .

We made our way to the "circus grounds," an amphitheater erected about a high raised stage. On one side sat our handsome, white-bearded emperor, sharp as an eagle, flanked by the duke and duchess. We were positioned opposite in seats of commensurate honor — either to separate us from the duchess or out of respect for Wisdom's unmarried status I could not tell, nor once the event began did I care. Oh, what a spectacle! A man juggled fire, and devoured it too, with a degree of finesse I could never have imagined. Another emerged from the stage depths with three tigers that he led through hoops and poses — I do wish Escoffier had been present to admire his stripy cousins, and to witness what a cat may accomplish. Then came a mob of boys hurling themselves through the air like so many monkeys, concluding with a tower six bodies high! They were followed by a lady snake charmer whose sinuous dance mesmerized not only the snake but every male in the audience; had she wand and powder, she could not have enchanted them more completely.

So engaged was I in this fantastic pageant that I tendered Dizzy only the scantiest attention, and realized too late that while other female viewers — and many male! — shrieked with fear and suspense at each breathtaking extravaganza, your sister's eyes only grew wider and her chin more determined, in that manner we both know too well; she had the visage of a man who after a lifetime of water at last tastes champagne.

Then — the floor pulled back to reveal the pièce de résistance: a golden orb that swelled until it filled the stage and rose into the vast circus tent. As magnificent as this globe was — balloon is far too meager to do it justice — even more mesmerizing was the young man posed atop it. Dizzy could not take her eyes from him, so it is all the more surprising that she alone did not react — though you may be sure that this old woman covered her head with a most unqueenly screech! — when he leapt off the structure and hurled himself toward us. Now I understood the purpose of the wide aisle wherein we sat, and saw the wire extending from his waist to the Globe d'Or. Coming to a stop directly before your sister, with great nonchalance he lowered his legs to the floorboards and, flourishing a golden rose, offered it to Dizzy with the emperor's compliments.

Dizzy accepted the rose with matching poise — her sang-froid all the more notable given that several women around us had fainted outright — and replied coolly that she should like to thank the emperor at once for his generosity — and held out her hand to the acrobat! Impudent girl! And he — with only a moment's pause at this doubtless unprecedented proposal—accepted her hand and pulled her from her seat into his arms! Before I could do more than gibber in fright, he was swinging her through the air, grasping her with absolute familiarity as her skirts fluttered about in a most unregal manner—the entire audience saw her legs almost to the knee!

So suspended from the basket of the Globe d'Or, they sailed together—not across the stage, as I had hoped, that she might be delivered to the emperor forthwith!—but in a great sweeping arc over the audience, the man's arms around her waist, her hands clasped on his. And then—I can scarce write the words!—Dizzy had the audacity (completely spontaneous I am sure, though it looked as though she had practiced for years) to point one slippered foot and, arching her back, extend one hand up to the sky as she rested against the man's shoulder, locking her eyes to his. Furthermore—they twirled! And as they did so, Dizzy leant back further still and somehow coaxed her skirts to flow most dramatically, accenting the circle they traced in the air—without a scintilla of concern that she might at any moment plunge to her death!

It was—I can use no other term—pure wantonness. That a princess would behave so—before the emperor and Farina! Had the option been possible, I would have fled, so profound my embarrassment and my well-justified fear that I would be blamed for Dizzy's renunciation of her position and all for which it stands.

At last—the escapade took only a few minutes, though my humiliation felt eternal—the two floated to a stop before the throne. Dizzy—yet holding the rose, I was glad to see; on top of all the other indignities she could not mislay a gift from the emperor himself!—with great aplomb curtsied to His Imperial Majesty.

For several long seconds the old man did not respond, and the audience—hundreds of people, from all ranks of life—sat breathless, goggle-eyed at this drama. The emperor had every right in his empire to condemn Dizzy's outrageous flouting of society's conventions. Her flippant presumptuousness could have—and, I will not deny, should have—earned her at the very least his disapprobation; imprisonment, or even banishment, would not have been out of the question.

Instead—to my surprise, and to the shock of Duchess Wilhelmina, who had observed her future daughter-in-law's performance with thoroughgoing outrage—he began to clap, his applause triggering a veritable thunder of accolades. The emperor, in fact, ordered a repeat showing at tomorrow's performance, which may explain why Wilhelmina departed the grounds soon thereafter with obvious ill-feeling, although Roger lingered to praise the princess's courage. For her part, Dizzy conveyed not an ounce of contrition; in observing her flushed cheeks and sparkling eyes I was reminded yet again of the fearless child who used to cavort, immune to our cries of horror and your tears, on the terrace railing.

While I held my tongue before the emperor, once we retired to the privacy of our rooms my ire knew no bounds. It will not surprise you to learn that Dizzy demonstrated no interest in my upbraiding, and indeed seemed deaf to my words — that is, until she hoisted a desktop ornament (tremendously ugly though that is no excuse for its destruction) and hurled it in my direction!

Not since childhood has she exhibited such tantrums, and I find myself at a loss as to how to proceed. Doubtless time will smooth this tension, and hours spent alone in her room will do her a world of good. Thanks to the emperor's fancy, she shall have one more opportunity to indulge her yen for flight or whatever it is she seeks in some acrobat's arms at the end of a wire. But after that: no more. Wisdom must devote herself to her station, and do so directly, for not all occupants of this duchy are as indulgent as the emperor, and he will not linger here forever.

Worse, as dismal finale to this mess, the girl Trudy — the "easy" member of my brood! — now weeps in her room as well! She dressed me for bed as if her world were ending, though my inquiries (tendered reluctantly, to be sure, for I have worries enough crowding my brow) produced little in the way of explanation. I gather she has some sort of family in Froglock and that a reunion had gone badly. It never rains but it pours, does it not — in this case a shower of salty tears!

I am relieved beyond measure that you remain in Montagne, Granddaughter — not only for the safety of our kingdom but because I fear that your very heart would have quit beating in mortification at your sister's performance at the circus and afterward. Speaking of which (and is this not a clever segue by your feeble old nonna?), how does your heart fare? I realize it is too soon for me to expect another letter, particularly given the speed and drama of the last delivery, but I dearly wish to be apprised. In the few moments this evening when I had opportunity to gather my thoughts, foremost has been joy at your happiness over your new suitor — and I hope I shall soon learn far more about him! I cannot wait to read of his family, his mien, his <u>name</u>! What a remarkable coincidence that he arrived in our kingdom the very day we left. Would that our departure from Montagne had been delayed that I might have met him — perhaps even served as Eros by introducing you both!

Let us hope that the mail riders find speed heretofore unknown and race to me your every happy word. Such favorable news will brighten considerably the gloom currently pervading our suite.

Your harried grandmother,
Ben

A Life Unforeseen

The Story of Fortitude of Bacio, Commonly Known as Trudy, as Told to Her Daughter

Privately Printed and Circulated

THAT NIGHT Trudy dreamt of Bacio, and Tips.

It wasn't even a dream, but a memory. Trudy had been eleven years old, Tips twelve, and the fever by that point was six months gone, the dreadful sickness that had orphaned them both. Eds the innkeeper had kept her on in her little room under the eaves, but he made clear that she'd have to toil, and toil hard, for her board.

That autumn forenoon, however, with the inn empty for a week and no customers but the sots who preferred the Duke's Arms to their own carping wives, Eds decided he needed a bit of a holiday. Handing Trudy a loaf of bread, he told her to go off and leave him in peace for the day. Which she did, scampering to the mill to share her good fortune with Tips, who immediately abandoned his task of sewing sacks, sticking his needle like a sword into the pile of burlap, and with a shout of laughter purloined from his brothers' larder a ham butt and a crock of fresh cider—the season's first pressing!—so that he and Trudy could go exploring.

Up they climbed into the Alpsburg mountains, higher than ever they'd been, until they stood in a bowl of sky so blue it took one's breath away, with the Alpsburg Pass in the distance, a great crack in the rim of the world.

There they found the glen: a flat little clearing, lush with wildflowers no higher than Tips's boots. It was so different, so magical, that it scared Trudy until Tips asked her to see if they were in danger. But they were not, because when Trudy looked about the glade she saw only happiness in her future. So they settled down with their picnic, and Trudy spread her apron for a tabletop, and Tips with his flint and little ax made a fire though the day was too warm to merit it, and they ate and laughed and told each other stories they both knew by heart. With their bellies full, they inspected every corner of the glen and found the spring, so small it was more of a weep, really, though the icy water tasted fresh as creation.

"We could live here!" Trudy exclaimed, and with that they went to work on a homestead. Tips chopped four little trees into timber for a lean-to against a south-facing boulder, while Trudy gathered pine needles for bedding and planned how to collect seeds and berries for winter, and how to store them.

It was, without a doubt, the happiest afternoon of young Trudy's life.

But, inevitably, the sun slipped toward the western peaks, taking with it the heat of the day, until both children were chilled, and Tips had to rub Trudy's hands between his own to warm them. Their little house looked cold and dark and very damp, and they remembered their own beds, and the people who would—if only for the loss of labor—notice they were gone.

"Let's go back," Tips said, and Trudy nodded, and they began to descend. But they did not know this route, for they had never traveled it before, and the path looked increasingly foreboding.

Trudy would not cry, but she had to bite her lip against the tears, and Tips squeezed her hand and told her not to worry, though they both knew he was worried too.

At last they came to a place where the mountain split in two directions, and the path such as it was split as well, and the children knew they would have to choose and that the wrong route might take them all the way to Pneu or Paindecampagne or off the edge of a terrible cliff that they would not even see until much too late, because the sun was setting now and it would be dark soon, without a moon.

Trudy began to sob.

Tips put his arms around her and told her not to fret, that everything would be fine in the end, though he wasn't exactly sure how—"Trudy! You can *see* home!"

"No, I can't!" Trudy wailed. "If I saw Bacio, we could walk right up!"

"No!" He shook her excitedly. "Look! Look down that path! What do you see?"

Trudy swallowed, and obediently looked, even though she couldn't see anything . . . except suffering. Sorrow and pain radiated up that path toward her. Reflexively she recoiled.

"Yes!" exclaimed Tips. "Now look down the other!"

No sorrow there, not that Trudy could see; only warmth, and the promise of sleep. She grinned at Tips, who was so clever to figure this out! "*That* way," she said simply.

Down they went, and at every branch, every possibility, Trudy saw the correct path in the repose awaiting her at the end. They stumbled into Bacio to find Eds with a torch calling their names, visibly relieved to see Trudy, and not just for her toil, either.

Tips went dashing off home—there was pain in his future yet, Trudy could see, though Tips didn't mind his beatings half so much as Trudy minded for him, and he spent every thrashing loudly protesting his innocence whether or not it was true.

She'd climbed into bed that night already planning their return to the glade, and the cottage that Tips would build her there someday. But then came work, and winter, and then the little swordsman came and took Tips away, leaving Trudy with no one.

When Trudy woke up in Phraugheloch Palace, it took her many minutes to remember where she was, and *who* she was, and that Tips was close—so close!—and yet even so, she could not find him.

She began to weep, and she did not sleep again that night.

A Missive From Tips

~~The Booted Maestro~~

Dear Trudy,

Ive just returned from ~~work~~ guard duty and found your letter saying youre coming to Froglock — please I beseech you DO NOT COME — I cant explain but I would be in great danger if you came ~~here~~ to this city. I will write more when I have time + will send you something very pretty, I promise. PLEASE — STAY IN BACIO — I BEG YOU —

— Tips

THE SUPREMELY PRIVATE DIARY
OF ~~WISDOM~~  OF MONTAGNE

Any Soul Who Contemplates Even Glancing
at the Pages of this Volume Will
~~*Be Transformed into a Toad*~~
Suffer a Most Excruciating Punishment.
On This You Have My Word.

Friday—dawn—

<u>Join me & I shall crown you queen of all the heavens</u>

All my existence has been a dream—a daze! Finally the fog has lifted—I see clearly at last!

I have not slept this night—my mind a whirl of impressions—confusion—wavering! But now I know. I would rather endure prison—death!—than the life I have been promised. Fashion—gossip—taxes—they interest me not in the least! I want none of it!

I saw him—our eyes met!—& Cupid's arrow pierced me through! I am in love. There are no words for this passion—I am on fire!

I shall crown you queen of all the heavens

I should flee—Roger appeals no more to me—to see him is to expire. Whither the emperor? In his trail I must follow.

Queen of all the heavens

Queen of all the heavens

Never have words moved me so! His whisper—his breath in my ear—I remember & I melt anew . . .

From the Desk
of the
Queen Mother of Montagne,
& Her Cat

My Dearest Temperance, Queen of Montagne,

Granddaughter, would that you were here this morn to comfort the two puddles of misery occupying our suite. You could work your magic (by which of course I mean exercise your compassion and tact) with sweet Trudy and offer her solace that I cannot — perhaps by exchanging tales of both your suitors! I managed to cheer her somewhat by promising to assist in locating a village boy now working in the emperor's court. I do wonder if I am somehow placing that poor orphaned child in the path of terrible, even unspeakable, harm. The child regards Dizzy with unmitigated dread, and given her past premonitions, I cannot but believe she has legitimate grounds for trepidation. Unfortunately, we must have Lady Fortitude serve attendance at tonight's Circus Primus; convention demands nothing less of a lady-in-waiting at her lady's last performance. Whatever trauma it is that Trudy fears, it will surely not impair Dizzy; we both know your sister's long history of spreading harm, however inadvertently or well-intentioned, yet always emerging unscathed.

Your sister . . . While Trudy altered another of Lady Modesty's dresses, Dizzy spent the morning staring out the window, clutching that silly golden rose. When a footman arrived to request her presence at an audience with Duke Roger, she was ill-mannered enough to blurt out "Who?" — as if she had never heard of her fiancé! Hastily I interjected an explanation, claiming — not inaccurately — that the princess was yet drained from last night. But if word of this insult should reach His Grace — or Her Grace! — I fear the repercussions. One moment —

An imperial page has just arrived with a missive requesting a private audience with the emperor. Dizzy leapt up, euphoric — until the page clarified that His Imperial Majesty wanted to see me. For a moment I feared Dizzy would burst into tears — she is clearly taken with Rüdiger, to an extent I would never have imagined possible. I must extricate her from this performance!

I will write later <u>demanding</u> information on your beau, and your life — but now, off to the emperor!

Your determined grandmother,
Ben

Memoirs
of the
Master Swordsman
FELIS EL GATO

Impresario Extraordinaire ✦ Soldier of Fortune
Mercenary of Stage & Empire

LORD OF THE LEGENDARY
FIST OF GOD
Famed Throughout the Courts and Countries of the World

&

The Great Sultanate

✳ THE BOOTED MAESTRO ✳

Written in His Own Hand ~ All Truths Verified ~
All Boasts Real

**A Most Marvelous Entertainment,
Not to Be Missed!**

I WOULD NOT be the first to assert that the arrival of *Wisdom* in Froglock provoked a most *unwise* reaction within the court, the emperor himself not excluded. My long-standing companionship with the great man permitted me an intimacy that few ever knew, and thus could I discern that the young woman's impromptu performance captivated him utterly. That a member of the royal class, born to buttress every tenet of society, should display such natural ability—occupying the ring as though trained from infancy for performance!—inspired profound reflection on both our parts. Not since my chance encounter in Bacio six years previous had I witnessed such inherent finesse, and my tumult of emotions included no small volume of regret that such a gifted soul was too highborn for the emperor's troupe.

Curiously enough, I faced another crisis in Tomas, who was suddenly overcome with a paralyzing and unprecedented malaise. While he strove to keep it locked within his strong young chest, I deduced that relations with his childhood friend in Bacio were not as amicable as they once had been. For years the boy had carried a torch for this innkeeper's wench, a flame I had not seen fit to extinguish, as it offered him comfort in lonely hours, and moreover their relationship of letters provided Tomas a modicum of security against unwanted suitors; on countless occasions I would hear him inform an amatory and determined lady or lass that, sadly, his heart had been promised to another. Yet I was beginning to find this pretense tiresome, for all childish passions dim with time, and I had encouraged him to respond more positively to such advances, particularly from women of high birth or deep pockets. He, however, refused.

His lack of interest in the fairer sex was in fact a subject I had resolved to broach afresh that very morn, but ere I could present this concern I was called to the emperor, and found

His Majesty with the queen mother of Montagne, the two of them deep in a discussion, curiously enough, on customs duties. Concluding their conversation as I arrived, the emperor requested that I give Her Majesty a tour of Circus Primus if I was not otherwise occupied. As his wish is but my command, I could not conceive of refusing.

The regal old woman occupied my attention for some time, and while I did indeed have multitudinous other responsibilities, I must confess I found her delightful, her flattering queries providing me copious opportunities to display my mastery of dueling, an expertise I now brought to Circus Primus. She expressed an extraordinary interest in the Globe d'Or and my considerable efforts to put to use the Sultan's Throne. (Here I pause in my transcriptions to curse yet again that damnable sultan, who in all his alleged generosity failed to include *instructions* with his gift; though I play the fool brilliantly, I prefer to do so of my own volition, and that bewildering collection of twigs and cables, the entirety as insubstantial as a kite, baffled even my substantial genius.) Displaying the seamless tact of the true patrician, she murmured sympathy for the ineptitude with which I was surrounded, and politely focused her attention elsewhere during this latest fruitless battle with that impossible device. Departing at last, she thanked me most graciously for my many anecdotes, and with haste did I finalize the night's performance, my acumen all the more visible given the brief time frame Her Majesty's visitation had imposed upon my genius.

FROM THE DESK

of the

QUEEN MOTHER OF MONTAGNE,

& HER CAT

My Dearest Temperance, Queen of Montagne,

Granddaughter, despondency fills me so, I scarce have
strength to pen these words. Oh, what I would give for a letter from you at this moment, some cheer to gladden my heart!
The mail riders, however, continue to arrive at the city gates
empty-handed, or so it is reported to me by Phraugheloch's
staff. I know you to be a most diligent correspondent, and
moreover — as I reassure my suspicious soul — I cannot imagine who besides myself would have interest in your news,
were anyone in Froglock so diabolical as to steal mail. Thus

stranded, I am left instead to cheer myself, and at this task, too, I fail utterly.

His Imperial Majesty, as you may recall, having called me to his quarters, once I arrived did not delay a moment in querying me about . . . taxation! Truly! Were the situation any less dire, his interest in finance would be most endearing. Apparently he considers Montagne a model of equitableness, and had prepared a great sheaf of questions, pausing in his interrogation only long enough to assure me that he "labors unfailingly for circus and empire."

Note, dear Teddy: circus and empire, not Princess Wisdom or Montagne! The consequences of your sister's slatternly exposure, particularly in regard to Farina —which she will ultimately be expected to rule! —concern him not in the least. Never once, no matter how I strove to turn the conversation, did I have opportunity to demand Dizzy be excused from performing. Instead, satisfied that he had extracted all possible information, he dismissed me without adieu. Gaping rather like a fish, I found myself returned to the tent's threshold with instructions to tour Circus Primus —a rare boon, or so I was informed by the guide inflicted upon me. Oh, was I distraught at my failure! And for the emperor to send me off like a schoolchild to busy myself admiring his dratted ensemble . . . He could not have flaunted any more clearly —and yet in so indifferent a manner — his authority over Dizzy and me and all of Montagne!

So it was that I most indignantly found myself conducted through the circus bowels by a short little man who has the highest opinion of himself of any individual I have ever encountered, the sole possible exception being Escoffier. This Felis el Gato — or, as he prefers, "the Booted Maestro" — possesses a voluminous knowledge of both Circus Primus and combat. He pontificated at length on an upcoming battle scene he was plotting while I stood, dozing upright like a cow in the shadows of the Globe d'Or. A makeshift brazier, bolted to the Globe d'Or's basket to heat the balloon, occasionally drifted ash upon us, and I would have far preferred scrubbing soot from the Globe's golden skin to feigning interest in this monologue. So desperate was I for diversion that I entertained even wicked thoughts of <u>magic</u> — how might my captor react were I, say, to wield Elemental Fire to singe off his waxed and well-perfumed goatee? (Rest assured, though, that I kept my fingers to myself, however much my brain craved otherwise!)

The Booted Maestro at last halted his oration to oversee several laborers attempting to attach a so-called <u>Sultan's Throne</u> to the Globe d'Or's basket, though why the stout old sultan would elect to sit midair, dangling like the last bite on a kebab, I can't imagine. I employed this time to converse with the acrobat who sailed your sister about the stage last night, intending to scold him for enabling Dizzy's extravagant display; I am glad I held my tongue for he proved to be remarkably charming. In fact he was quite eager to share the secrets of his magical flight, showing me the Globe d'Or's block and tackle that effortlessly lowers and lifts him, and describing how he calculates the length of wire needed for each jump. He was about to reveal the harness beneath his clothes when he caught my baffled look. "You seemed so worried about your granddaughter," he explained, "that I wanted to assure you she is safe." Oh, irony! I had not heart to explain it is her <u>reputation</u> and not her bones for which I fear! He even presented me with an extra scrap from the skin of the Globe d'Or, assuring me that the patch was otherwise useless, as no one could get a needle through it — one small reassurance that perhaps the Globe itself is immune to punctures. Let us hope so, at least until Wisdom survives her display this evening.

Yes, Granddaughter, her performance will happen. I cannot halt it. Hoping to bend his ear, I even returned to Rüdiger's quarters after my tour, but the emperor was otherwise occupied with the duke and duchess. My grief doubled when I returned to our suite to find your sister stitching with unprecedented enthusiasm her white gown for the upcoming performance. The blush that came to her cheeks when the page arrived to escort her to "practice" made my heart sink all the further.

Needless to say, I refrain from discussing with her the wonderful news of your romance, for infatuation smothers empathy, and your sister bears too little of that virtue as it is. But trust me, Teddy: you are in my thoughts. While my inked words require five days to reach you, I hope that their spirit crosses forthwith the plains of Farina and the mountains of Sottocenere to touch your heart. I await your correspondence with bated breath and beating heart, and can only hope that the delay means the letters, once arrived, will be even more elating.

Your useless grandmother,
Ben

THE IMPERIAL ENCYCLOPEDIA
OF LAX

8TH EDITION

Printed in the Capital City of Rigorus
by Hazelnut & Filbert, Publishers to the Crown

ELEMENTAL SPELLS

Chemistry, meteorology, mineralogy, hydraulics: these and myriad other natural and applied sciences grew from mankind's understandable curiosity about the four natural elements. This same impulse, unfortunately, has also led to distasteful shortcuts and outright chicanery. Into this latter class fall the Elemental Spells. First cataloged by itinerant storytellers during the reign of Gustav I, this alleged magic purportedly gives its wielder the ability to create elements supernaturally via the spells of Elemental Fire, Elemental Water, Elemental Earth, and Elemental Air. The Kingdom of Montagne, sullied for many generations by association with witchcraft, was the initial locus of this myth, though similar tales emerged in other corners of the empire; raconteurs in the Sultanate of Ahmb describe a flaming-haired demoness who draws water from the sky, an understandable illusion for that arid country. In the last century two separate and respected imperial committees devoted to the eradication of fantastical thought proved the impossibility of the Elemental Spells, which subsequently faded from popular consciousness and today serve as little more than an amusing anecdote, when they are remembered at all.

The Gentle Reflections
of Her Most Noble Grace, Wilhelmina,
Duchess of Farina,
within the Magnificent Phraugheloch Palace
in the City of Froglock

Never in my life have I been so insulted—it is a travesty that the emperor has ruled for nigh on three decades with such unmitigated incompetence!

Today he had the audacity to assert that Farina <u>impoverish</u> itself—simply to satisfy his latest imbecilic whim!

I should expel him at once—<u>and</u> cancel Roger's engagement to that cheap little tart, after the spectacle she made of herself last night—but Montagne is almost in my grasp!

Therefore—it pains me beyond measure to scribe these words —I have made a <u>concession.</u>

I must pay a penny to earn a pound, for the wealth of Montagne will soon be ours—<u>if</u> the emperor acquits himself properly.

I have no faith in the man—or should I say the <u>showman</u>—but he has proved to be as pathetically malleable as every other disaster of virility inflicted upon this suffering earth—I must not consider my hardship <u>too</u> severe, as I have once again applied another's weakness to Farina's advantage!

I believe I shall enjoy tonight's performance very much indeed.

Memoirs
OF THE
Master Swordsman
FELIS EL GATO

Impresario Extraordinaire ✦ Soldier of Fortune
Mercenary of Stage & Empire

LORD OF THE LEGENDARY
FIST OF GOD
Famed Throughout the Courts and Countries of the World
&
The Great Sultanate

✳ THE BOOTED MAESTRO ✳

WRITTEN IN HIS OWN HAND~ALL TRUTHS VERIFIED~
ALL BOASTS REAL

A Most Marvelous Entertainment,
Not to Be Missed!

TO THIS DAY I consider "The Demon Vanquished" one of the crowning moments—if not the absolute pinnacle—of Circus Primus, and upon closing my eyes can still recall every step and stroke of that superlative act. Such dramatic narrative! Such dazzling swordsmanship! Such romance! Such pathos as the demon descended, arms akimbo, in the throes of death! Most remarkably, this extraordinary spectacle was created in only a few short hours. While dueling (of which I had no small experience, to be sure) and acrobatics both held a long and honored role within the circus, it was the recent acquisition of the Globe d'Or that permitted the most brilliant combination of these two arts; on this momentous evening the elements, graced with *Wisdom*, fused at last.

To best capture my genius, I shall describe the scene through the eyes of an awestruck spectator.

The stage opened with Princess Wisdom—outfitted most beguilingly in a gown of white—arranged motionless on a bier. Guarding her was a frightful, red-caped demon who frolicked menacingly about his prisoner. In a burst of exultant music, a winged angel entered stage left and with gleaming sword confronted the fiend, who drew his own black blade in response. With a clang of steel, the foes clashed: lunge, feint, riposte, transfer, coup! Footwork, bladework, as only a master swordsman such as myself could manage. And then the demon took flight—pursued by his virtuous opponent! As they fought mid-air, the gasps of the audience revealed that every viewer saw too well the peril inherent in this battle. One wide stroke could slice a wire and send either performer smashing to his death; thus was every eye doubly captivated. No, *trebly* captivated; I cannot but acknowledge the contributions of Her Highness, for even recumbent and immobile, the princess held the stage.

Finally the angel with mighty blow slew the demon, who

floated down, expired. The angel descended as well and with great passion studied the immobile princess, tenderly (though this gesture was most definitely *not* in the script) brushing a hair from her forehead, his face close to hers. Instantly the princess awoke. Rising to her feet, her hands never leaving the angel's, she began to dance. He joined her, and so passionate was their pas de deux that the two rose bodily into the heavens, until they were not dancing but flying, the princess's skirts trailing like a gossamer chorus.

I had seen enough of their hasty practice to believe Wisdom's innate grace and fearlessness would disguise her dearth of training, and once again my extraordinary perception proved true; her blazing passion heightened further and further still the power of that airborne waltz. When the two ultimately returned to the stage, the princess curtsying most gracefully to His Majesty, the applause that greeted their finale was louder and more sustained than any I in my long life had ever heard. What a contrast this moment served to the chaos immediately following.

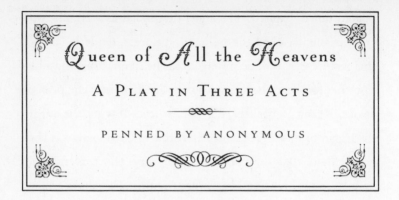

Act I, Scene viii.
Circus Primus, with full audience.

Wisdom is posed asleep on the circus stage, guarded by a demon.
Enter Rüdiger IV, Benevolence and Fortitude,
and Wilhelmina and Roger with retinue.

BENEVOLENCE [*to Fortitude*]: Observe the princess immobile. Let us pray she remains so.

FORTITUDE [*aside*]: How can Princess Wisdom be so lovely and yet so foreboding?

WILHELMINA [*to Rüdiger*]: You will not forget our pact, Your Majesty.

RÜDIGER [*to Wilhelmina*]: I could not, Your Most Noble Grace . . . Let the performance begin!

An angel battles the demon onstage and midair.

ROGER: O! Wisdom! I would defend you if I could!

RÜDIGER: The demon is vanquished! A brilliant performance; I am so proud . . . And yet with a touch they leave the script. I am not so pleased with that part.

Wisdom and the angel dance together onstage and midair.

BENEVOLENCE [*aside*]: Caution, Granddaughter, caution! The passion you display may yet destroy you.

WILHELMINA [*to Roger*]: With her every touch, the princess cuckolds you. This is not performance but burlesque, and a mockery of this duchy and your rule.

Wisdom and the angel land, then bow to Rüdiger.

WILHELMINA [*to Roger*]: We strike while the iron is hot ere the iron flees us. Observe my handiwork, Son.

RÜDIGER: As emperor of this great land, I have many duties, none of which pleases me so much—excepting of course this marvelous circus!—as officiating at the union of man and wife. Therefore, without further ado, I announce that Duke Roger and Princess Wisdom will wed tomorrow.

WISDOM [*aside*]: So soon! Horrors! My heart shall break!

FORTITUDE: O! Angel! I know your face!

WISDOM: Speak not with such familiarity to my true love—my angel, Tips!

TIPS: Is it—my eyes deceive me—it is my first and oldest friend. Trudy!

FORTITUDE: Tips, I have found you at last—in the arms of another!

Fortitude faints. Wisdom faints.

ROGER: My darling princess! Now I may race to your rescue!

TIPS: My first love, and my true love, both fallen . . . What awful grief have I brought upon us all? O woe!

WILHELMINA [*to Rüdiger*]: You bind that harlot to my son by dusk tomorrow, or all of hell will suffer for it.

PART III

HEARTS BREAK!
LOVERS PART!
VILLAINY,
UNMASKED,
REVEALS
ITS FOUL VISAGE!

In Other Words:
ALL IS LOST!

WILHELMINA
THE ILL-TEMPERED
(CONTINUED)

That Wilhelmina considered the marriage of Roger to Wisdom of paramount importance may be seen in the concession she secretly granted the emperor: the elimination of Farina's tolls on imperial mail riders. (That she preserved the tolls for all other traffic illustrates her negotiating prowess.) The coupling of the duchy to Montagne constituted the cornerstone of her grand plan to elevate Farina to regal status, that her family might then make claim to the imperial throne. Nor was Rüdiger IV—an elderly campaigner by this juncture, and perhaps too concerned with Circus Primus—in any position to confront Wilhelmina's ambition. Farina's contributions to the imperial purse could not easily be disregarded, and the duchy controlled the very crossroads of the empire. Were Wilhelmina to close its borders, imperial trade would halt outright. The emperor therefore acceded to Wilhelmina's demand and commanded that the nuptials take place immediately; his act of officiation—a great honor, and irrevocable—would lock Montagne to Farina forever . . .

From the Desk
of the
Queen Mother of Montagne,
& Her Cat

My Dearest Temperance, Queen of Montagne,

Granddaughter, life here passes from bad to worse — or I should say from <u>worse</u> to <u>perfectly dreadful!</u> The circus performance — how long ago it seems, yet not an hour has passed! — was brilliant, I must grant it. Your sister, despite spending much of the act prostrate, had full command of the stage and performed with grace and great dignity, all things considered — truly I should be overjoyed . . .

Were I not <u>distraught.</u> For poor Dizzy had not a moment to rejoice in her success before the emperor announced that she and Roger are to wed — tomorrow! You should have seen Wilhelmina — the woman looked as smug as Escoffier with two mice — she has orchestrated this! I cannot imagine what she promised Rüdiger in return for his cooperation, but the emperor stated that he himself will lead the ceremony! So much for the fortnight of balls and the grand procession that _she_ has always demanded . . . Instead the wedding now suggests a sword-point elopement. Dizzy, on hearing the emperor's words, promptly _fainted,_ which I suspect was only a ruse, though Roger received much approval from the crowd for carrying her from the stage in his arms.

Yet — I dread writing these words, though you and I have certainly discussed this situation, and indeed predicted it — your sister has no longer an ember of interest in the duke! To be sure, their bond has always baffled us; while the duke managed to convey enthusiasm for the girl as well as the title, Dizzy seemed most interested in the adventure Roger promised — a rather flimsy hook on which to hang one's heart, particularly given that Roger stands closer to stolid than stirring. Well, Dizzy has now come to this truth. She has fallen utterly in love with the acrobat with whom she performed — the young man who flew her through the circus heavens last night! And he regards her with the same burning fire! 'Tis no surprise that Wilhelmina insists on an immediate wedding, for she — rightly, no doubt — fears her quarry will soon flee.

Making matters worse still—for why burn house alone when stable can blaze too?—poor Trudy is absolutely overcome. She also fainted at the circus, and as we returned to our suite grew near hysterical with grief. While I in no way claim to understand completely what has transpired—you may be certain my mind is occupied with other matters!—I did manage to deduce that the acrobat who delivered Dizzy to our feet was none other than her childhood friend found at last. Given that no one could miss the devotion he expressed for the princess, Trudy feels justifiably spurned. To see one's love appear on angel's wings admiring another . . . That would be pain indeed. To his credit, the young man did attempt to speak to her but was drawn away by his master, the Booted Maestro, costumed quite appropriately as a demon.

Would that I had energy to comfort Trudy, but I am far too caught up in this pending debacle of a wedding. While I grasp Wilhelmina's desire for haste, I have no understanding of the motives behind it. Why is it so imperative that Dizzy wed Farina? I cannot see through Wilhelmina's plot, and this unnerves me profoundly. Were Dizzy queen, I could comprehend the duchess's greed . . . But the throne is occupied by you—a most healthy specimen! I far preferred the Duchy of Farina when it was ambitious and stupid!

I apologize for unburdening myself so, but I have no one else to whom to turn. If only the oysters had spared more of our entourage — even Lady Patience would be a boon, as she can at least manage a cool cloth for my brow . . . Your mother and father were both so enviably levelheaded — how I wish they were present now! In my desperation I have even consulted Escoffier, but he only assures me that a good ear cleaning will cure all my worries. How marvelous 'twould be if life were so easy!

I pray that by the time you receive this missive, both explanation of and solution to this crisis will have been obtained and you will have the luxury of laughing at my panic. Your next letter, I must not doubt, races toward Froglock even as I write. Would that it could fly, for I cannot wait to hear more of your romance, your suitor, your success at governance, and all the other happiness that one may find — far from the bounds of Farina!

Your distraught grandmother,
Ben

THE SUPREMELY PRIVATE DIARY

OF ~~WISDOM~~ ᵥ *Dizzy* ᵥ OF MONTAGNE

Any Soul Who Contemplates Even Glancing
at the Pages of this Volume Will
~~*Be Transformed into a Toad*~~
Suffer a Most Excruciating Punishment.
On This You Have My Word.

Friday—v. late—

I am lost! The emperor—the emperor himself!—announced I am to wed tomorrow!!! Hearing those words I nigh perished on the stage! I am quite sure I did faint—regardless of Nonna's sniffing over my behavior—she sounded as stuffy as Teddy—& Roger truly was dashing as he bore me away—in its own way as exciting as the performance—the applause so real . . .

But why bother writing of applause when I have such pain! I cannot marry Roger no matter how solicitous he may be—how handsome—how rich—because my heart belongs utterly & forever to Tomas. My true love. My one & only Tips. The words he whispered last night as we sailed through the air—his arms holding me tight—

Join me & I shall crown you queen of all the heavens

—never in my life have I felt so alive—so full of love!—& he as well! This afternoon while practicing—that officious little el Gato may be vain as a cat always twirling his mustache but he certainly knows how to fashion a spectacle!—every moment with Tips felt—perfect. Every touch—every word—perfect.

He has no fear—no pretension—no preening! He has traveled the world—has met the breadth of humanity from pauper to sultan—he knows the emperor & tolerates with absolute equanimity el Gato's boasting & bossing—& throughout all this his soul—so clearly!—remains unpolluted.

He is modest AND confident—has any man ever managed this duo? Certainly none I have ever met!

He never once mentioned my beauty or my face or my title— he saw only me.

He wants me.

Were it possible I should flee these chains of state & spend my life in his arms. We need only the air—the wire—& I am complete—I would rather perish with Tips than live with Roger—I cannot marry the duke!!

Yet the emperor's word is law! What am I to do? To think that all my life I have craved excitement—but this is not exciting —this is misery.

Misery pure & absolute.

A MISSIVE FROM ^Tips^
~~THE BOOTED MAESTRO~~

Dear Trudy,

Youre a lady-in-waiting—I didnt even know! When I saw your face this evening all I could think was how beautiful ~~you are~~ that lady is—+ then I realized it was ~~Trudy~~ you! I know Ive been ~~lying~~ not telling you everything for ~~six years~~ a long while—every time I wrote about being a <u>soldier</u> or a <u>guard</u> ~~I was fibbing~~ it cut me so much inside—its such a relief to say the truth at last! But I had to ~~lie~~—dont you see?—its the only way I could remain in Circus Primus. Hans + Jens would never release me to a <u>circus</u>—theyd say I was only a <u>clown,</u> that a circus is a <u>waste of time + money,</u> that its full of <u>boasting men</u> + <u>women no better than they should be</u>—you know theyd speak so. I love this life so much—I am ~~good~~ ~~ackomplished~~ <u>good</u> at this! You saw me, didnt you? I was made for ~~performing~~ this, not for grinding flour + counting coins. But I was afraid if I said the truth, ~~you would~~ it would somehow get to them—I know you can keep secrets but still, one slip + my life is over. I would rather die than return to Bacio!

There is something else too—I know my ~~words~~ ~~explanation~~ ~~excuses~~ words here will not do, I wish I could talk to you—there is another ~~girl~~. I swear—on our mothers graves!—that Ive never loved anyone else—the words I wrote you were <u>always</u> true— until last night. Now my heart is split in twain—half to you, half to ~~Princess~~ Wisdom. She is like no ~~girl woman~~ one I have ever known! To see her is to know life as it should be—+ yet I ~~love like~~ care for you as well. Youve always been the center of my world.

Im lost—Im wretched—I dont know what to do. Trudy, I beg you—please understand I never set out to hurt you—now I fear Ive hurt you most of all!

With care—+ love—

—Tips

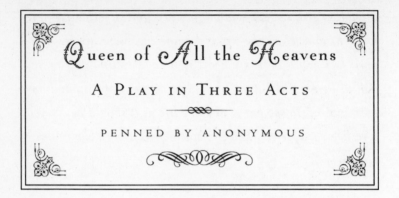

Queen of All the Heavens

A PLAY IN THREE ACTS

PENNED BY ANONYMOUS

Act I, Scene ix.
Wisdom's suite in Phraugheloch Palace.

A knock. Fortitude, weeping, opens the door.

FOOTMAN: A letter for Lady Fortitude.

FORTITUDE: I thank you ... O Tips! ... It is as I feared—you love another! O my love, you have broken my heart!

Fortitude exits the suite, weeping.
Enter Wisdom, weeping, and Benevolence.

WISDOM: How shall I survive this? I know I must marry, but tomorrow ... 'Tis too soon!

BENEVOLENCE: What scheming do these nuptials hide? I smell strategy behind the haste—strategy most diabolic.

A knock. Benevolence opens the door to Roger.

ROGER: Good evening, Your Majesty. Have you no maid or footman to perform this labor?

BENEVOLENCE: Honest work should never trouble honest people . . . Good evening to you, Your Grace. How fare you this night?

ROGER: I came to inquire as to the well-being of my betrothed. If there be any succor to offer, please do not delay in communicating how best I should convey it.

BENEVOLENCE: His Majesty's announcement has quite overwhelmed my granddaughter, who fears too little time to prepare her wardrobe.

WISDOM: Yes! I have not yet a gown suitable to wed a duke.

ROGER: Our love needs no cloth to secure it! I have burned six months to be your groom; 'tis a light in my heart that I shall be yours tomorrow.

WISDOM [aside]: But do I wish to be yours in return?

BENEVOLENCE: If six months you have tarried, why dash now? I must confess I find baffling this need for dispatch.

ROGER: We would the emperor's blessing . . .

BENEVOLENCE: Yet Rüdiger lingers in Froglock, as well he should for such enthusiastic crowds. Many details yet require resolution —the terms of your style, for example. Does not Her Most Noble Grace take issue with "Duke and Princess"?

ROGER: 'Tis of no account! My sweet mother thinks only of what is best for our family, as do I.

BENEVOLENCE: In wedding Wisdom you will have a new family to defend.

ROGER: I prefer to think of Wisdom joining our greater whole . . .

BENEVOLENCE: As a drop of rain is absorbed into a broad ocean?

ROGER: Precisely!

WISDOM [aside]: Heavens preserve me! I shall be drowned!

BENEVOLENCE: I had anticipated a more compassionate response to my metaphor . . . I must ask outright: what schemes do you hatch for this beloved girl?

ROGER: Schemes? I take offense! It will be only glory for us both —glory that we but deserve!

WISDOM [aside]: We, we, always it is two! Where am I to be found in this equation?

BENEVOLENCE: 'Tis my experience that a ruler's call for glory leads to many men's pain.

ROGER: You wish Farina to remain a duchy, undistinguished? Easy words for a queen of a kingdom!

BENEVOLENCE: My granddaughter shall not wed a man more zealot than peer.

ROGER: It is the emperor's decree—you will defy that? I thought not. Fear not, Your Majesty, for the princess's royal status is most valued by my mother and myself. I depart, my betrothed; tomorrow, my wife.

Exit Roger.

WISDOM: I do not like that man!

BENEVOLENCE: Nor I . . . Yet what other resolution can prevail?

Enter Escoffier the cat.

WISDOM: We are not entirely without power . . . You have capacities, handsome Escoffier, do you not?

BENEVOLENCE: No! We made a solemn vow—upon the death of another!—that we would abstain forever from magic.

WISDOM: Yet this union shall cause the death of me!

BENEVOLENCE: Surely we may yet devise a natural solution. O dear cat, what are we to do?

Memoirs

OF THE

Master Swordsman

FELIS EL GATO

Impresario Extraordinaire ✦ Soldier of Fortune
Mercenary of Stage & Empire

LORD OF THE LEGENDARY

FIST OF GOD

Famed Throughout the Courts and Countries of the World
&

The Great Sultanate

✳ THE BOOTED MAESTRO ✳

WRITTEN IN HIS OWN HAND ~ALL TRUTHS VERIFIED~ ALL BOASTS REAL

A Most Marvelous Entertainment, Not to Be Missed!

☜

SADLY, the audience's most fitting veneration of "The Demon Vanquished" was cut short by the emperor, who—to my pique, I cannot deny it—interrupted the thundering adulation to proclaim that the princess would wed Duke Roger the very next day! This unexpected news sent the princess into a swoon—

performed quite artfully, if I may say. Duchess Wilhelmina appeared thoroughly satisfied with the emperor's words; clearly the woman deduced what so many astute observers, myself most of all, had already observed: her son's betrothed now preferred a well-trained circus acrobat. Sensing that the spotlight had faded from our act, with a flourish of my red demon cape I withdrew from the stage with my apprentice. The uproar from the emperor's announcement affected the show for some time, and I fear the tigers, with that innate animal ability to sense unease, were too unsettled to perform. Nor did Tomas appear for his usual act upon the Globe d'Or despite the three runners I sent to seek him out, and so I was forced to stage the Jug Juggler in his stead, and a poor substitute he proved.

Experienced as I am in the torment which love wreaks, I sought Tomas out upon the show's conclusion, and, as I had expected, found the young man in the throes of romantic agony. While he recognized too well that Wisdom, royal born and promised to another, could never be his, he had yet dreamt of enjoying his sliver of paradise a few brief days more. Exacerbating this tragedy—as I learned in sobs and fragments while he raged about his chamber—his childhood sweetheart, that tavern wench to whom he remained so interminably loyal, was in Froglock this very minute, employed as none other than lady-in-waiting to the princess! And she, in witnessing the fervor of Tomas and Wisdom, underwent her own most brutal humiliation—made all the worse by her having up to that moment believed her love to be a *soldier!*

I could only marvel at the extraordinary drama of this romance, and my mind straightaway commenced concocting how best to put it to the stage. My theatrical instincts, however, did not prevent me from simultaneously endeavoring to set Tomas's heart at ease. He, I deduced, had already sent Trudy (a name I recalled all too well from countless previous conversations) a missive explaining his predicament and apologizing for the suffering he had inflicted, and while his promptness in this regard should be commended, the gist of his correspondence as he summarized it for me was not close to the more lyrical words of which an experienced beau would doubtless have been capable.

So it was that I urged the young man without fail to approach this Trudy, and with voice and manner express the thoughts that with ink and paper he so patently had not. I advised such a tactic well aware of the lad's magnetism, and the fact that he wielded his dark brows and lashes as another might a bouquet of roses. For a woman had but to see the young man—as so often I had witnessed these past years—to fall under his spell. Such was his inherent goodness that never once had Tomas employed this facility for the infliction of suffering, and I knew in my heart that the maid's pain would only be eased by his physical presence. With kind words he could explain the necessity of passing himself off as a soldier given his two brothers, who together had as much appreciation for art as an eel would for mountaineering. Though Tomas begrudged the falsehood, I had forever exhorted him to persist, explaining again and yet again how this one small *misdeed* permitted all his great *deeds* (a lovely example of the phenomenal word craft of which I am capable, particularly when my genius is called upon in the heat of debate). Now, conversely, I employed the same brilliant logic as I soothed him that this cloud of misunderstanding had a bright silver lining in that he could at last speak the truth and relate to the girl his many adventures and accomplishments these past years.

Much gladdened by my excellent counsel, the lad promptly set out, though heedful of my warning that his appearance in Phraugheloch would doubtless sit ill with the duchess. I, on the other hand, delighted that my sagacity had once again produced such an assuredly successful outcome, settled myself in my private tent for some well-deserved slumber.

A LIFE UNFORESEEN

THE STORY OF FORTITUDE OF BACIO, COMMONLY KNOWN AS TRUDY, AS TOLD TO HER DAUGHTER

Privately Printed and Circulated

WRETCHED TRUDY! No one in the history of Lax had ever been so miserable. To discover in one instant that Tips had been misleading her for six years *and* that he now loved another . . . It was only a terrible dream, Trudy almost convinced herself—and then came his letter, confirming all her worst fears.

She could not bear, not for another instant, to remain in that horrid suite, not with the princess in the next room—with Trudy expected to wait upon her! Horrid Montagne and its horrid people stealing other lasses' sweethearts! Trudy would never speak to them again. Not even to Nonna Ben, however nice the old woman might sometimes appear to be, at least to Trudy's face . . .

Weeping with sorrow and rage, Trudy fled into the palace proper, thankful beyond measure for the empty corridors, the vast rooms and marbled staircases echoing away into silence, their few occupants focused on their own tasks and thoughts.

Every Phraugheloch staff member and attendant, it seemed, was busily preparing for the extravagance of tomorrow's royal wedding—a wedding Trudy would not be attending, however unseemly that might appear. All she wanted was to go home. Put a scarf over her hair, her old cape over her shoulders, and go back to Bacio.

But . . . but . . . she could not.

In her anguished wanderings, Trudy realized with a wheeze of dread, she had become totally lost. She had not a notion where in the palace she was. The corridors faded one into the next: here a mirror, there a palm tree standing forlorn and lonesome in an enormous embellished pot, elsewhere a ceramic vase taller than Trudy herself. And everywhere, firmly shut doors.

Even if she could find the palace entrance—which seemed very far away indeed from wherever it was that she now stood—she would not depart Froglock without her few possessions. But where in this architectural monstrosity was their suite?

She must not panic . . . Nor need she panic, she realized suddenly, for her sight seemed to work here, quite tidily, in fact. If one corridor filled her with trepidation, then she obviously should take the other.

Which was precisely what she did.

Trudy moved through the hallways with growing confidence, pausing only to step aside when others approached; tonight of all nights she had no appetite for prying eyes and disparaging whispers.

On she trekked, climbing staircases and creeping down dimly lit corridors, surprised she had traveled such a distance unwittingly . . . and then stopped. She had to stop, for the corridor ended, quite abruptly, at a great pair of doors bearing a polished brass plaque:

CHANCELLOR OF FINANCE
ENTRY INVARIABLY & MOST VEHEMENTLY FORBIDDEN
WITHOUT THE EXPRESS WRITTEN PERMISSION
OF HER MOST NOBLE GRACE
THE DUCHESS OF FARINA

THE SUPREMELY PRIVATE DIARY

OF ~~WISDOM~~ *Dizzy* ∨ OF MONTAGNE

Any Soul Who Contemplates Even Glancing
at the Pages of this Volume Will
~~*Be Transformed into a Toad*~~
Suffer a Most Excruciating Punishment.
On This You Have My Word.

Friday—v. late—

My life grows ever more dreadful! Roger has just departed—I
cannot imagine what I ever saw in the man. He does not love
me—he loves only my title & his infernal glory. Were it not for
the emperor's edict I should run away this very night with Tips
& a few possessions in a sack—like that girl in the story—&
find my fortune as I might—perhaps another circus would take
us—

Yet why waste the ink to write these words—there is no hope.
I even suggested—such is my desperation!—that Nonna &

I chance magic—but she v. wisely set me straight! Now she weeps as well—the only time I have ever seen her cry save for dear Mama.

O Mama—why did you have to do that! You were so good at so many things—you did not need to fly! It should have been me on the broom that fateful night—I have a head for heights—it is on ground that I fail—as I fail now!

Nonna is right—magic brings only jealousy & outrage & despair. Besides how could a magic broom help—or the Elemental Spells? We have no power against the will of Rüdiger IV—& that beastly, beastly Wilhelmina!

O! A sound—at the window! It is my love come to me at last!

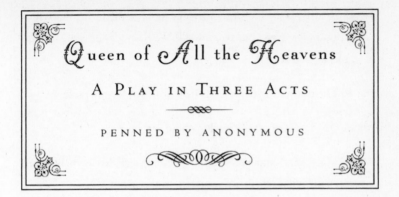

Queen of All the Heavens
A Play in Three Acts
PENNED BY ANONYMOUS

Act I, Scene ix (cont'd).
Wisdom's suite in Phraugheloch Palace.

Benevolence paces. Wisdom writes at her desk. A knock.

BENEVOLENCE: A ghost, atop our other woes!

WISDOM: It is my love—my angel!—come to me at last!

Enter Tips.

TIPS: I mean no fright, Your Majesty, for I am no ghost, only a humble performer. I beg you: I must have a word with Lady Fortitude.

WISDOM: What? Not me?

TIPS: I must explain myself to her—perhaps my words will offer comfort.

BENEVOLENCE: She has fled, I fear.

TIPS: To Bacio? 'Twill be my undoing!

BENEVOLENCE: I know not her location, or intent . . . But tell us, fair lad, why tread our windowsill? We have a door quite serviceable; indeed several.

TIPS: The duchess, I suspect, has little stomach for my presence—

WISDOM: So? Let all the world behold our love!

TIPS: Moreover, I know this building's casing well, having many times traversed its façade in service to the emperor.

BENEVOLENCE: As spy?

TIPS: I must confess it. Love demands naught but truth.

WISDOM: O my darling, you are too brilliant! How could I ever love another?

BENEVOLENCE: A spy . . . a vocation of which we now have desperate need.

WISDOM: O darling, you must spy for us!

TIPS: I am not sure of this . . .

Enter Escoffier the cat.

BENEVOLENCE: I am certain the duchess schemes even now . . . Know you her location?

TIPS: Without fail . . . Yet no human could enter that room unnoticed.

BENEVOLENCE: Nor shall any human do so.

WISDOM: O Nonna Ben! You would not!

BENEVOLENCE: Spelling lost me my daughter, but perhaps it will preserve hers.

Exit Benevolence holding Escoffier.
Wisdom and Tips embrace.

WISDOM: A moment of bliss! I cannot deny myself!

TIPS: Nor I . . . Yet I confess I do not follow Her Majesty's thinking. How does spelling lend assistance—have you no dictionaries?

WISDOM: Think not upon it. Simply deliver Escoffier to the duchess's chamber; he shall see to the rest.

Enter Escoffier, who leaps onto Tips's shoulders.

TIPS: Gadzooks! He is like no creature I have ever known! Does this cat possess intelligence?

WISDOM: Far more than that; he doth provide it. Fly, my love! Be safe! Be true!

Exit Tips and Escoffier through window.

WISDOM: I shall keep the casement open in expectancy of their return . . . My grandmother slumbers behind closed door, preserved in a veil of enchantment . . . We have profaned our vow! Yes, yes, I am a sorceress—I do confess it—but one imperiled by misery eternal. O, how I pray these Dark Arts illuminate my gloomy plight, and light a path to resolution . . .

THE IMPERIAL ENCYCLOPEDIA OF LAX

8TH EDITION

Printed in the Capital City of Rigorus
by Hazelnut & Filbert, Publishers to the Crown

DOPPELSCHLÄFERIN

Also known as "the sleeping double," the Doppelschläferin is yet another now-disregarded shred of magical lore from the Kingdom of Montagne. That the name is feminine—the standard, masculine phrase should be Doppelschläfer—reiterates the kingdom's long association with female witchcraft. The Doppelschläferin is part of the legend of Queen Virtue, founder of Montagne, who was said to have devised it while held prisoner by the Pots de Crème Giants; the spell (she claimed) allowed her to split into two identical bodies—one unrousably asleep, the other conscious and cogent—that could be reunited at will, often many years later. Several of her heirs professed, when it was yet acceptable to invent such tales, to have improved upon the spell by employing pets, most often cats, to operate as their doubles, viewing the world through the animal's eyes while their human body remained "asleep." As false as this myth most patently is, the legend had strategic advantages: the Montagne army once feigned sleep en masse, and the sight so terrified the approaching Drachensbett forces that the soldiers broke ranks and fled. The fairy tale "Cat Whiskers" contains the last published reference to a Doppelschläferin, and it concludes with both the witch and her Doppelschläferin feline burnt at the stake.

From the Desk
of the
Queen Mother of Montagne,
& Her Cat

My Dearest Temperance, Queen of Montagne,

Granddaughter, I have broken my pledge and returned to magic — violating every vow I made to you and Dizzy and the memory of your dear mother. And would that I had not — for the truth I learned is far worse than anything I could have conjectured!

Tonight Duke Roger paid a call to our suite and in heated conversation revealed his true self, which is only a more polished variant of his mother's selfish grasping. Dizzy now professes that she would rather die than wed him. I do not believe she will take her life, but I would not wish this life upon her.

No sooner had His Grace departed than Dizzy's new love appeared at our window — fittingly enough for an acrobat! — hoping to speak to Trudy, or Lady Fortitude as he sweetly termed her. His good intent crumbled to despair when he learned that the lass had departed the suite for points unknown. Our conversation did reveal that the lad had no little experience as spy — also fitting for an acrobat in liege to the emperor! At once I glimpsed a faint path out of our horrible predicament: in learning Farina's true intent, we perhaps might thwart it. I recognize too well that eavesdropping in and of itself is villainous; to conduct such depravity through veil of magic rightly brings upon witchcraft every censure the empire might devise. However dismayed you must be in your grandmother, know I am more dismayed in myself. Yet if I could have perceived a solution beyond sorcery to this wretched dilemma, trust I would have exploited it forthwith.

Oh, Granddaughter, you cannot imagine my agony as I whispered those enchanted phrases. With every word, I recollected more vividly that fateful night, the reckless exuberance of Dizzy and myself, and your mother's breezy assurance that she would be <u>fine</u> and <u>safe</u> upon my broom, her eagerness to experience at last the magic of flight after so many years of yearning . . . <u>I should have known better!</u> You are wise beyond measure to keep your two feet firmly planted upon the ground and to accept, however reluctantly, that you lack both the power of magic and its pain.

Thus incorporated with my feline partner while my creaky old body snored abed, I then contravened the Empire of Lax's most cherished laws and mores. With little urging from Dizzy, Tips escorted noble Escoffier — unaware of the cat's recent enlightenment — to the duchess's privy chamber. There, as I had suspected, she sat plotting with her son and several others. Tips was fortunate enough to find a window cracked ajar, and though the young man could not hear the conversation within, supple Escoffier slid through this opening as a black shadow and traversed her suite undiscovered to the table, heaped with papers, where the schemers conspired. To my delight, the duchess had with her that miserable little dog, and so Escoffier's silent leap to the table's center had the effect not only of frightening the faction almost to death but also of setting the dog off as a fuse lights a firecracker, with easily as much noise. Adding insult to injury, Escoffier then lounged in a most possessive and feline manner across the documents, a stroke of brilliance that even in my fear and grief cheered me immeasurably.

The duchess at once made to strike Escoffier a vicious blow, but her son deflected her swing, pointing out that a pet from Montagne should not be harmed. "Not yet, anyway," sneered Wilhelmina. "I shall sleep much easier once this marriage is sealed and the abdication complete."

Yes, Granddaughter, you read correctly: <u>Abdication</u>! Oh, Teddy, an awful conspiracy has been concocted, and Wilhelmina and her son fully expect you will quit your throne — within the week!

Would that I could spare you this terrible reality — alas, I cannot. Instead I shall report my findings swiftly; the sooner pain is felt, the sooner it may pass. Darling, it appears — and from the confident and informed manner with which these connivers schemed, I cannot but believe they speak the truth — it appears your suitor, sweet-tongued though he may be, is in actual fact an agent of the Duchy of Farina! And his only task has been to win your love that he might convince you to leave Montagne forever — and by so abdicating, pass the throne to your sister! Is that not horrible?

Wilhelmina is a wicked, wicked woman; it was all I could do not to hurl Escoffier at her to scratch out her eyes. If only I could be there to sit with you and comfort you in your grief, reassuring you again and again that someday, me dear, you will find true happiness.

Numb with shock at this loathsome discovery, I hastened back to our suite and released myself from Escoffier that I might read again your description of this alleged suitor — and yet your letter was nowhere to be found! Such correspondence I treat most carefully, securing it within a locked casket, and to discover it missing devastated me utterly. I am certain that it has been stolen, and moreover I cannot but suspect that your more recent missives have met a similar fate — at the hands of a villainess whom we can both readily identify — that I might remain ignorant of your plight.

Please, Granddaughter, much as it will crush you, you must imprison this rogue at once. I shall return as hastily as I can, lingering in Froglock only long enough to see to Dizzy's safety.

Please, I beg you: protect your nation and your throne!

Your panicked grandmother,
Ben

A Life Unforeseen

The Story of Fortitude of Bacio, Commonly Known as Trudy, as Told to Her Daughter

Privately Printed and Circulated

HANCELLOR OF FINANCE? Oh, goodness dear.

Trudy turned about, baffled. Her sight had never failed her like this. And what precisely was this corridor, anyway? Every door—and there were so many!—had a label: RECORDS J–L; RECORDS Z+; UNDERSECRETARY OF DOMESTIC PROTOCOL; STATIONERY, DIPLOMATIC; MOST SECRET SERVICES (and how secret could they be, Trudy wondered, with the name engraved for all to observe?); LIBRARY OF LAW. The library door, remarkably enough, stood ajar—the first open door Trudy had seen that night—and as she passed, a quavering old voice called, "Anna, you're late!"

"I beg your pardon?" Trudy asked, remembering that with her recent weeping she must look a fright.

But the old man was too busy to look up for more than a brief second; certainly not long enough to recognize that she was not in fact the negligent Anna. He wrestled with an armload of rolled documents, a lit pipe in one hand.

"May I help?" Trudy asked, fearing he might set the room ablaze. Perhaps the man could lead her back to the main entrance . . . or at least out of this bureaucratic labyrinth.

Bleating complaints about the indolence of modern youth, the graybeard loaded her with parchments, leaving himself unburdened except for the pipe. He glared at her. "You're not Anna!"

"No, I—"

"If you're not Anna, then you're someone else," he added, with flawless logic. He shuffled toward the door, then turned. "Aren't you coming? Are you dim?"

What a thoroughly unpleasant individual, thought Trudy. How could her sight have led her *here?* "I am—Lady Fortitude—" The last time she might ever require that horrid fakery!

They walked without speaking for some time, the old man muttering to himself. "Montagne, eh?" he stated at last, glancing at her sideways. He had hair growing out of his ears and curling off the tip of his nose. Trudy did her best to look elsewhere.

"No, I'm from—"

"Damned ridiculous system you've got there. In Montagne."

"Oh?" Trudy offered after a space.

"Female succession! Damned ridiculous. A country needs a king. Just like a woman needs a man."

I had a man—almost, Trudy thought, struggling to keep from weeping.

"And sloppy! The whole legal system's sloppy. Are you sloppy?" He fixed her with a beady eye.

"Ah, no . . ."

"That's one thing I can't stand. Sloppiness. You write a law, it's meant to stand! No damned loopholes. You put a loophole in, someone will find it. Someone with a legal mind," he added, tapping his temple. "Not like those damned sloppy Montagne lawyers."

"Oh. I'm sorry to hear that."

"Well, I'm not. It's not right, a country without a king. It's not right *ever*. You hear me?"

"Ah, yes . . ." Trudy wondered how long she would be burdened with this crabby mossback. Her urge to escape the palace was now overwhelmed by her desire to escape his spiteful presence. Besides, she knew where she was now—that portrait, of the baron who looked like he'd just drunk bad milk, was only a short distance from their own rooms . . .

"Yes, well, Montagne knows it too. Or they will soon enough." The curmudgeon poked his stinking pipe at the parchment below Trudy's nose.

She looked down. There, amid the gold leaf and wax seals and embellished foreign words of what was without doubt an extremely important manuscript, was the neat signature of "Temperance, Queen of Montagne," and next to it a flamboyant scribble that could only belong to Wisdom.

No sooner did Trudy see this document, however, than the old man snatched it from her arms.

"It's for Her Most Noble Grace. I've a meeting with her —her and the duke—and they won't like that I'm late." He clutched the stack of parchments to his bony chest and glared at Trudy. "What are you doing here, anyway? I wager you're a spy—a Montagne spy. You're certainly not a lady."

A spy? Never had Trudy heard something so ridiculous, so utterly . . . dim. No, she was not a spy, and most certainly not one from Montagne. How she wished she had never heard of that horrid country. How she wished she had never come to Froglock! . . . Well, she would manage. She would more than manage. She would show them all—even Tips!—that this orphan was a survivor.

She glared at the old man, her irritation for once obliterating all thought of decorum. "You're right. I'm not a lady. If you want to know the truth, I'm a kitchen maid." And with that she raced down the corridor to collect her belongings and return, at last, to Bacio.

THE IMPERIAL ENCYCLOPEDIA OF LAX

8TH EDITION

Printed in the Capital City of Rigorus
by Hazelnut & Filbert, Publishers to the Crown

CUTHBERT OF MONTAGNE

The life course of Cuthbert of Montagne is surely without parallel in the Empire of Lax. Born to a charcoal burner in the then-Kingdom of Drachensbett, the boy from a young age exhibited a precocious aptitude in the natural sciences, particularly silviculture and mycology, and after studies abroad returned to establish the Department of Botany at the Universität Drachensbett, which had been founded after Drachensbett's absorption by its smaller neighbor Montagne. While on the faculty, he was introduced to Crown Princess Providence; it is safe to say that their courtship stunned the kingdom. Once married, Cuthbert absolved himself completely from politics, remaining on the faculty of the Universität Drachensbett to study his beloved fungi. When Providence's mother, Benevolence, relinquished her title of queen to retire and enjoy her two granddaughters, Providence was crowned ruler, and Cuthbert, following

Montagne tradition, named prince consort. Nine years into Providence's reign, Cuthbert perished while tasting unnamed mushrooms, a death that even his grieving family agreed was more than fitting. To honor her late husband, Providence posthumously elevated Cuthbert to the unprecedented "king regnant," in effect transforming his position to that of sovereign. Such a radical alteration to the monarchy was accepted without challenge, though it had profound repercussions for the next generation of Montagne's rulers. Providence died mysteriously three years later, and the throne passed to their daughter, Temperance. *Cuthbertii,* a previously undiscovered subgenus of alpine mushrooms, is named in Cuthbert's honor, as is the savory mushroom pie *Cuthbert en croûte,* now the national dish of Montagne; the phrase "Cuthbert it," as in "to leave something," implicitly to perish or decay in a beneficial manner, was coined by Drachensbett students, and the court of Montagne to this day serves mushrooms with every banquet course, though recently making an exception for the dessert ices.

From the Desk
of the
Queen Mother of Montagne,
& Her Cat

My Dearest Temperance, Queen of Montagne,

Well, Granddaughter, I have at last a full explanation for Wilhelmina's insistence on this wedding, and now my blood runs cold. There is not a moment to spare — Montagne hangs in the balance! For Farina intends not only to remove you from the throne, but <u>Dizzy as well!</u>

I had just finished a missive to you, calling for a page to include it — <u>quite securely!</u> — in the morning's mail, when Trudy returned to our suite. She could no longer contain her misery and insisted on returning to her village. Nothing I said, nor Dizzy, to her credit, could dissuade her. While packing her belongings, the girl described her hours in the palace — most significantly her encounter with a misanthropic legal scholar more conversant with our laws than any attorney in Montagne. It took all my wheedling to coax the details of their encounter from Trudy, who was most interested in her own swift departure and cared far less about the curmudgeon's plotting than that she had met him at all. "I should have seen such unhappiness," she kept wailing — an admission, however inadvertent, of her clairvoyance. I did not wish to upset her further by verbalizing her secret; otherwise I would have soothed her with the reassurances that magic by definition defies reason and that elucidation would doubtless emerge in the fullness of time. Perhaps the child bears a connection to Montagne, though how <u>our</u> ultimate happiness might improve <u>hers</u> I cannot figure — and at this moment the happiness, indeed the very survival, of our kingdom hangs in limbo!

Oh, Teddy, I fear that your mother's efforts to honor dear Cuthbert will rain dishonor upon us all. Her declaration elevating him from <u>prince consort</u> to <u>king regnant</u> apparently contains a "loophole" — the precise word used by that disagreeable legal expert — that will allow others — Roger, to be precise — to rule as <u>king</u>!

How many times have you and I pondered why Wilhelmina would permit her son to marry a younger princess when they both so desire the Kingdom of Montagne. Well, I now, so sadly, know the answer: Wilhelmina intends to push you aside (by abdication or <u>even worse,</u> I fear!) and crown her son king — apparently the reams of parchment the battle-axe sent us to sign included a cunningly worded document orchestrating this precise outcome! I do not need to explain that once her claws are in Montagne, we shall never be free again, and our country will dwindle into yet another province of voracious Farina.

Given Rüdiger's edict tonight, it is manifest that the wedding will transpire tomorrow; your sister's fate is sealed. But you can — you must! — safeguard yourself, and our land. Please, Teddy, <u>keep yourself protected at every moment.</u> If you do not, all is lost.

I pray this letter reaches you on eagle's wings, or angel's.

Your terrified grandmother,
Ben

The Gentle Reflections
of Her Most Noble Grace,
Wilhelmina, Duchess of Farina,
within the Magnificent Phraugheloch Palace
in the City of Froglock

⟡

What pleasure it gives me to read others' mail!

I shall preserve here the two latest missives from that witch-queen to her sniveling granddaughter—they form a singular addition to their correspondence.

Have I not always suspected that the queen engaged in sorcery? —now at last I have the <u>proof!</u>—written in her own hand!

Once I possess Montagne, I shall see that miserable crone of a witch burned and her diabolic black feline stuffed and mounted.

It perturbs me not in the least that she and her cretinous spawn now know my plan—for they have no capacity whatsoever to stop it.

My agent in Montagne has served the world well by destroying all correspondence from that idiot young queen with her mawkish jabber of love (the very thought makes me gag!)—he writes that Temperance is now in his thrall, and that she meekly agrees abdication is her best and only means of demonstrating her devotion to him.

How I value a man so adept at destroying female confidence.

This wedding cannot happen soon enough.

A Missive From ~Tips~

<del>The Booted Maestro</del>

Dear Trudy,

Im sitting outside the duchesss window if you can believe it — Ive written you from stranger places but never I think from any-place so <u>high</u> — I do hope if I fall that whoever finds <s>my body</s> me will make sure you get this letter — if they can read my moonlit scribbles, that is.

<s>I dont know what to say Im trying to figure out</s> —

I have never in my life cared for anyone the way I <s>do</s> care for you. You always say <u>Im all you have</u>. But for my entire life, youve been all that I did. You had a mother at least who loved you, but my father + brothers never loved me at all.

Without you Id have <s>nobody</s> no one — not just these past six years, but ever since I can remember. There have been so many times when I was alone — or worse when some girl <s>or lady or gentlewoman</s> was begging for my company — offering coins as if I were a carnival ride! — + it was only you, + the memory of you, that kept me from despair.

I never told you about ~~the circus~~ Circus Primus, + I feel so ~~bad~~ awful about that. ~~I know~~ Felis ~~said~~ told me not to but its not his fault, its mine. I didnt ~~trust~~ have enough faith in you. More than that, I was afraid if Hans + Jens found out, I wouldnt be able to forgive you.

But now I know I was wrong.

~~Dizzy~~ Wisdom—I know you dont want to hear about her + I dont blame you one ~~wit~~ whit—but I ~~have to explain~~ must try to explain at least. Because for the last day Ive been mad with grief + heartache. From the moment I saw the princess, I was in love. Even before she spoke! I dont know why! Except that I noticed ~~the very first thing~~ she is not proud.

I so ~~dislike~~ hate pride! Its a ~~problem~~—its a <u>sin</u>—in far too many people—+ not just noble-born. You + I have both met beggars in tatters + rags who live only to lord their rank over the beggar beneath them. My brothers put as much energy into <u>lowering</u> themselves as many gentlemen put into promotion, claiming they are "common born" + "not with airs"—+ it is so clear that they do this not out of love for equality, but from envy + hatred + <u>pride!</u>

But Dizzy accepts every person she meets, + if she judges it is for ability + enterprise, not position or birth. She cares as much for the lowest roustabout as she does for the emperor—I ~~obzerv~~ saw this myself during rehearsal, when his majesty appeared and she alone did not rush to greet him but stopped to thank two stagehands for their efforts and ask them to demonstrate their machinery, with no thought of the <u>emperor</u> and how she should be fawning over him as everyone else always ~~does~~ seems to—she so clearly has no interest in rank, and what a ~~joy~~ relief that is!

Its not just that either. Ive always thought I could find contentment in every situation, + Ive ~~prided~~—well, there it is, I have pride too! much as I try to avoid it. I have <u>prided</u> myself on this skill. But Dizzy outdoes me. She finds more than contentment —she finds happiness. Even hanging ½-smothered from a cable while they worked hours on spotlights she was laughing + ~~I know I sense~~ I can tell she would face any horror to find the bliss inside it.

+ she is brave! Braver than most men, + she doesnt even ~~know~~ show it. Once the cable slipped + dropped her ½-way to the stage, + she didn't say a word.

I dont pretend to know <u>true love</u>—Felis talks of it all the time, + has been married twice just since Ive known him—+ yet his <u>eternal bliss</u> lasts only a few weeks. Romance has no guarantee of forever!

But family—loving family—that survives time + broken hearts + any length of distance.

You are my family—before + now + always.

I am so sorry for what Ive done to you. For the truths Ive kept from you, + my lack of faith in you. I hope you can forgive me, but I understand if you cant.

With all my love forever,

Your family,

Tips

THE SUPREMELY PRIVATE DIARY
OF ~~WISDOM~~  OF MONTAGNE

Any Soul Who Contemplates Even Glancing
at the Pages of this Volume Will
~~Be Transformed into a Toad~~
Suffer a Most Excruciating Punishment.
On This You Have My Word.

Saturday—

I am being fitted—three seamstresses toil even as I write—I
shall make a v. presentable bride if not a willing one. Escoffier
sits in my lap tho I suspect he wishes mostly to coat my gown
(gift of Wilhelmina) in cat hair—his own small attempt to
cheer me. With each minute the wedding draws closer as the
scaffold approaches a doomed criminal—or is it the criminal
approaches the scaffold? It does not matter—suffice to say that
it is bad!

Trudy has departed. I cannot say I blame her—she returned
to our suite last night to find me pacing—the explanation that

I was "awaiting Tips" she misunderstood & she refused to believe Tips originally came to our rooms to see her. I had no idea he mattered so much! Nonna begged her to stay but the girl insisted on returning to Bacio . . .

And then Tips returned with a letter to give her but she was already gone.

And now so is he.

I am so scared.

The Gentle Reflections
of Her Most Noble Grace,
Wilhelmina, Duchess of Farina,
within the Magnificent Phraugheloch Palace
in the City of Froglock

❧

Terrible news!

The witch's "lady-in-waiting"—a vain little tramp who clearly expects her hair to forgive her low birth; Handsome has far bluer blood than she ever hopes to—has fled Froglock! Eastward!

If that fool by some miracle of competence manages to reach Montagne—this cannot be allowed!

As I told my most brilliant agent—at the time speaking of Montagne, but the dictum applies generally—petty laws are designed for petty men; those who would achieve greatness must act greatly.

I myself—a gentlewoman of impeccable breeding—could never condone anything so vulgar as <u>murder.</u>

Yet not only Farina but Montagne, and indeed humanity as a whole, would benefit from the removal of one empty-headed young woman.

Or several, should the situation warrant it.

We would not be the first to barter a soul for a throne, and while such a decision is most certainly burdensome, it is not without ample reward.

Ample reward indeed.

MEMOIRS
OF THE
MASTER SWORDSMAN
FELIS EL GATO

Impresario Extraordinaire ✦ Soldier of Fortune
Mercenary of Stage & Empire

LORD OF THE LEGENDARY

FIST OF GOD

Famed Throughout the Courts and Countries of the World

&

The Great Sultanate

✳ THE BOOTED MAESTRO ✳

WRITTEN IN HIS OWN HAND~ALL TRUTHS VERIFIED~
ALL BOASTS REAL

A Most Marvelous Entertainment,
Not to Be Missed!

I AWOKE brimming with satisfaction at my excellent performance the night before, both onstage and as counselor to young Tomas. All of Froglock was abuzz over the duke's wedding, the imminence of the event adding a piquant urgency to the day. The emperor contributed further spice by ordering the Globe d'Or transported outside, beyond the protection of the great circus tent, that he might observe the couple's reception procession from the air. Naturally it was well within my authority to point out the imbecility of such a demand, for every fool in Lax knew that this most precious and delicate object had never once been exposed to the elements and would moreover be snatched away by the first gust of wind; only a suicide would take flight in that perilous basket, its coals poised to spill fiery death, its anchor line sundering at any moment, sending vessel and rider drifting away as helpless as a dust mote, impotent against the merciless heavens. Yet this dictate came not from just any fool but from the emperor himself, and I am far too faithful a servant ever to question His Majesty's judgment.

Thus I diligently toiled, chiding the roustabouts whenever they criticized the great man's faculties, and with no little effort did we extract that golden sphere from its sanctuary. I myself tied the three—note the number, dear reader, my prescience once again sensing the catastrophe to come—*three* cables that secured the Globe d'Or to terra firma. Heartened that I had done everything possible to assure the safety of Rüdiger IV—and to this day I comfort myself that my considerate actions played no role in the subsequent tragedy—I returned to my chambers that I might prepare myself for the upcoming nuptials.

While the gray day may have dampened the enthusiasm of some of the arriving guests, I myself have far too much regard for the establishment of wedlock ever to allow a few lowering clouds to dim my keenness for a wedding—certainly my many unions were every one of them a day of great celebration, though I cannot speak as positively about the months then ensuing.

Given that the emperor himself would lead the service, I could don naught but my best, and quite a dashing figure I cut when at last I had luxury to examine myself in the full-length glass that accompanies me always. The slashed velvet doublet and hose of lilac and indigo contrasted most pleasingly with striped stockings of mustard and jade, while my cape's scarlet lining flashed delightfully whenever the polychrome brocade fell open. The peacock plume in my toque—a well-deserved gift from the sultan of Ahmb—highlighted further the iridescence of the ensemble, and I must say I could scarce draw my eyes from the magnificence before me.

Imagine, then, my surprise when I discovered Tomas still abed! And my stupefaction when he informed me that he had no wish to attend the wedding! When I probed most gently into the outcome of his nocturnal parley with Trudy, he retorted only that he was "done with love"! Perhaps their conversation had not proceeded as artfully as I had predicted. I implored him to arise from his cot and dress, for the wedding was not an hour hence and the emperor expected his most cherished performer (here taking the liberty of certain hyperbole, as certainly *one* other member of the cast was more valued than Tomas) to attend the blessed event. He could not allow his infatuation with the princess to cloud his judgment, and his future.

Untouched by my pleas, he refused. Not even my offers

of coins—of the show's finale—swayed him, and he expressed not a modicum of sympathy for my fate should he abandon his responsibilities at this most consequential moment.

I had lingered as long as I dared. Devastated as I was by this turn of events, my long career had hardened me to such slings and arrows, and I accepted with worldly toleration the pain that would crush another man. Imploring him one last time to reconsider his impetuousness, I departed, as disappointed in his rash juvenility as in the fact he had not offered one word of praise on my attire. So it was that I hurried, alone, to the cathedral.

✻ ✻ ✻

Volumes have been penned on that pivotal ceremony, sovereigns and scholars and common men pondering its every nuance, the significance and consequences of the vows—the toast—the kiss ... It is therefore only fitting that I improve upon that wealth of speculation by providing the world an unbiased chronicle, for I was—I state modestly—a superlative if not perfect witness, observing unblinking every detail of that event, from commencement to tragic conclusion, with an informed and learned eye.

Experienced as I am at the performance of matrimony, I delighted in the setting, for the Froglock cathedral is a magnificent edifice, its marbled chapels and gilded statuary incorporating the full spectrum of architectural styles and artistic décor. The duchess's servantry had toiled through the night to gather every available Froglock blossom, which they to the best of their ability presented in vases and garlands about the altar and along the aisles. Banners emblazoned with the duchy's coat of arms hung from every column, and it was perhaps in response to this that the emperor hung his own seal on a curtain behind the altar. I confess that I studied this display with a certain pang, for—and I write these words in full acknowledgment of Rüdiger's ability, and his many years as showman and ruler—the effect was not as artistic as I would have achieved, the imperial indigo needlessly darkening the sanctuary (or "stage," if I may introduce so temporal a word into a place of worship) wherein the ceremony would take place.

It is remarkable as well—and here I reiterate that I communicate as only a witness, and in no way seek to criticize the event—that a function of such import had so few participants. His Imperial Majesty officiated without assistance, while Duke Roger was presented only by his mother, and Princess Wisdom by her grandmother, bride and queen both with grim visages. Her Most Noble Grace, on the other hand, radiated satisfaction and performed her ceremonial duties with alacrity. Had I been closer, I would have prodded Princess Wisdom to smile occasionally, and smooth the wrinkles from her brow; sadly, Duke Roger had not such skill with words but could only in the manner of grooms through the ages look worriedly from bride to mother, clearly agitated about how henceforth to mediate between the two.

The emperor spoke the ritual from memory, having performed it countless times, several for me, and while his words on this occasion may not have carried the same passion that they did at my nuptials, he held the attention of every observer. Roger, too, with firm confidence uttered his vows, his voice reaching the farthest corners of the colossal edifice. Wisdom, I am sorry to report, for I had heretofore held her showmanship in high regard, stumbled repeatedly, and once failed to speak altogether, so anxious did she seem, so that Rüdiger was forced to repeat himself, though he handled this with finesse.

The vows completed, the ceremony moved to a tradition unique to Farina, in which the groom's mother presents wine to the couple that they may toast each other, and her. The tradition (it is sometimes insinuated) demonstrates that hereafter the bride will be serving the every need of her husband and mother-in-law; surely such was not the case at this wedding, however smug Wilhelmina may have appeared, and however quickly it was that she trotted across the stage with her two goblets, thrusting the smaller into Wisdom's limp hand. The princess consented to wet her lips, but Wilhelmina lifted the goblet again and insisted that the girl as custom dictates swallow every drop. Only after Wisdom, struggling, achieved this did the duchess proffer the larger bejeweled vessel to her son and nod in satisfaction as he drained it.

Rüdiger then escorted the couple—Wisdom stumbling slightly—onto a low dais directly before the imperial coat of arms, driving home with gesture as well as word the supremacy of empire over duchy. He spoke at length on the history of Lax and of Farina's tradition of subservience. The duchess absorbed this narrative with a visible scowl, Queen Benevolence with apprehension, while Wisdom, ever paler, wrung her hands, and Roger radiated naive delight. The finale of the emperor's speech is recorded here verbatim, as I transcribed it for use in a future production.

"And so with a kiss will this ceremony be concluded," the emperor stated. "The kiss is the seal, rendering immutable the vows so recently exchanged between this princess and this duke"—here looking from Queen Benevolence, who after a moment nodded, to Duchess Wilhelmina, whose scowl transformed into a triumphant smile. "If there be anyone who challenges this union in the name of statecraft or love, speak now, or for ever after will these two souls and their realms be bound."

The emperor paused to look across the crowd, and every man held his breath to listen. I heard a step and a rustle, and my heart beat fast at the drama of my young Tips so theatrically claiming the woman he loved . . .

But no, it was only a banner rustling, and the step belonged to no one. My brilliant imagination had once again bested my reason. Onstage, Wisdom bit her lip, her eyes squeezed tight. I can only infer the great emotions surging within her lovely young bosom.

Rüdiger continued: "Gentlemen and ladies, men and women, children among you, family members"—here gazing firmly at Wilhelmina—"remove your hats and withdraw your handkerchiefs that we may all of us mark this marriage." He nodded at Roger, who, beaming, stepped toward his bride. For a long moment the princess stared into his face. With a deep and expressive sigh, she leaned forward and touched her lips to his.

At once the hush erupted into deafening cheers, as everyone present—including even Her Majesty and Her Most Noble Grace—tossed hat and handkerchief into the air. What a glorious moment and what a fantastic spectacle, that multitude of cloth and feathers (though none of the hats quite so glorious as mine) fluttering through the air like a heavenly flock of birds. How we applauded! How we saluted! For who does not enjoy a wedding, even one with a bride as reluctant as this?

It was only after some minutes that the great room grew quiet, and I began to ponder the length of that matrimonial embrace, the duke clutching his bride so tightly. And then—oh, how my heart breaks to write this!—Roger turned, Wisdom in his arms, and howled in sorrow, his anguish silencing the last revelers.

"She is dead!" he cried. He held her out to the assembly, and as one we gasped to observe her head loll back and one shapely arm swing dully. "She kissed me and she died! Help me! Help me, someone! Help me to restore Wisdom's kiss!"

THE IMPERIAL ENCYCLOPEDIA
OF LAX

8TH EDITION

*Printed in the Capital City of Rigorus
by Hazelnut & Filbert, Publishers to the Crown*

WILHELMINA
THE ILL-TEMPERED
(CONTINUED)

As per Wilhelmina's demands, Rüdiger the following day married the Duke of Farina to Wisdom of Montagne. Wisdom's collapse at the exact moment of the couple's nuptial kiss remains one of the great unsolved mysteries in the history of Lax. Alchemic investigation of the goblet and the wine with which the princess had enacted the traditional Farina wedding toast revealed no trace of poison, nor could the empire's physicians and autopsists explain her expiration. Yet all evidence pointed to Duchess Wilhelmina, who had filled the goblet, presented it to the bride, and forced her to empty the glass. Despite her most vehement protestations of innocence, the duchess was tainted forevermore by the scandal, and it is believed the term "the willies" derives from a vulgar threat to "give someone the Wilhelmina treatment"—

that is, to poison them. However disgraced she may have been to her countrymen and peers, however, Wilhelmina was never tried for the crime; indeed, she succeeded in her objective of binding the Duchy of Farina in perpetuity to the throne of Montagne. Nor, it emerged, was this the full extent of her far-reaching and devious stratagem . . .

A Life Unforeseen

The Story of Fortitude of Bacio, Commonly Known as Trudy, as Told to Her Daughter

Privately Printed and Circulated

RUDY WAS SO TIRED that she could barely remain upright. A night without sleep and a full day of travel had left her with a brain of sand, and in her exhaustion and strain she saw danger behind every sapling and low-hanging cloud. So it was that she crept to the kitchen entrance of a roadside tavern and begged a bowl of soup before the evening rush. With food in her belly, she'd have strength enough to push on to the next lodging place, for she had three more days of walking to reach the border of Bacio.

Wearily she sat to eat, laying beside her the sack holding her few clothes, the earrings, and Tips's letters—all her possessions in the world. Staff soup it was, and well she knew such amalgams of leftovers and yesterday's meat, in this case gamy if not yet turned, though she was too spent to care. She ate quickly, struggling not to dwell on Tips and the aching hole he had left in her heart. How would she bear Bacio? His letters, the promise of his return, of their union, had made her life—if one could call so colorless an existence a *life*—worth living. Without him, she had nothing.

Hoofbeats pounded toward her, and suddenly horses and men crowded the graveled yard. Trudy gasped: these were the duke's men-at-arms, the very soldiers who had tried to help her find Tips! Oh, she could not bear the embarrassment of being recognized! She pulled tighter the kerchief around her head and drew her rough cape close.

The soldiers, however, did not notice the girl cowering in the shadows, but instead tramped through the main entrance calling for victuals. A babble of voices rose within as guests questioned the new arrivals. Had they any news of the duke's wedding?

The wedding had taken place, confirmed one man. But his voice was heavy, and somberly he reported that the princess had collapsed at the service, and that certain busybodies with no loyalty to their state whispered of poison.

Wisdom poisoned? Trudy could not believe it! Certainly she did not care for the princess (to put it mildly), but she would never wish her ill, or . . . or dead. This was shocking news. Shocking and awful.

The man continued speaking, silencing the jabber. He and his men had raced from Froglock on a crucial mission. Had anyone seen a red-haired lady-in-waiting? This . . . female had departed Froglock before dawn, and Her Most Noble Grace feared the lady carried information she should not. For the safety of the duchy—of the empire—she must be found, and returned to the capital to be tried and punished!

Listening to this, Trudy quaked in fright. Against her better judgement, her legs trembling, she eased herself up until she could see inside the tavern. There, past the harried kitchen staff, she managed to catch sight, just for a moment, of the speaker, who so filled Trudy with horror that it was all she could do not to shriek.

She must run—fly!—escape this place! If they dared assassinate a *princess,* what might they do to a simple orphaned . . .

No, she could not panic! Not with her life hanging in the balance. Clawing her kerchief ever tighter about her face, she slid down the wall, praying with every fiber of her being that the movement not be spotted.

Gingerly she set the empty soup bowl on the doorstep, and gingerly she lifted her sack. Oh, how she wanted to sprint away! But such haste would draw the attention of every soldier within the tavern. Her only hope lay in anonymity, in making herself so nondescript that these murderous men could not possibly pay her notice.

And so Trudy, though her heart screamed to bolt straightaway, instead dawdled across the courtyard and out to the road.

Up the muddy way she trekked, keeping to the shadows as much as she could, forcing herself not to look back. She could imagine their probing eyes studying her, wondering who that lass might be, why she traveled alone, and what was under that kerchief . . . Stop! she scolded herself. If the soldiers didn't dispatch her, her own frenzied terrors would.

She scrutinized the steep hill before her. If she could just make it to the crest, that would be success enough—she could see it. Then she could take refuge in the woods without raising alarm by creeping off the road. Once over this hill, she knew, she would be safe . . .

Walking as quickly as she dared, panting at the effort, Trudy began to climb. The breeze intensified—and her kerchief blew off! Trudy lunged, but already the accursed wind had snatched it away, and snatched her hair as well, sending her long locks—brilliantly red, even in the cloudy gloom!—fluttering in all directions.

Trudy struggled to restrain her hair. Now released, however, every strand whipped about maddeningly. How could they not notice her with hair flying like a crazed flag! Hot tears of frustration stung her eyes—she was at wits' end—and then she heard a distant shout. She had been spotted!

Blind with panic, Trudy stumbled, then began to sprint. Another shout, and another—now she raced full-out, pounding with the desperate illogic of a doe run to ground—

A great blow caught her broadside, knocking her breath from her body.

Memoirs
of the
Master Swordsman
FELIS EL GATO

Impresario Extraordinaire ✦ Soldier of Fortune
Mercenary of Stage & Empire

LORD OF THE LEGENDARY
FIST OF GOD
Famed Throughout the Courts and Countries of the World

&

The Great Sultanate

❋ THE BOOTED MAESTRO ❋

WRITTEN IN HIS OWN HAND~ALL TRUTHS VERIFIED~
ALL BOASTS REAL

A Most Marvelous Entertainment,
Not to Be Missed!

GREAT DRAMA has always compelled my full attention, and I bore no small connection to beautiful, delicate Wisdom, having revealed her innate artistry only the previous day. While others grieved the loss of their *princess*, I could not but grieve as well the loss—so senseless! so theatric!—of one of the grandest performers, if only for a night, of the grand Circus Primus. For no sooner had the Princess of Montagne wedded handsome Duke Roger than she collapsed . . . poisoned!

Most repugnantly, the perpetrator of this fiendish act—not an observer could deny—was none other than Her Most Noble Grace, Duchess Wilhelmina. *She* had pushed the goblet into the girl's reluctant hand, had handed the *other* goblet to her son. Were I to stage a poisoning (not that ever I have, though on several occasions I have been sorely tempted, most especially with my third wife, and well would the harridan have deserved it), I could not have orchestrated it more artfully. Nor did it require the genius of the great Felis el Gato to find Her Most Noble Grace's denials too fervid, particularly in light of the animosity and calculation that had always marked her relations with Montagne.

The poison operated most sinisterly. Never in my remarkable life have I encountered such a malevolent toxin; the many physicians summoned to the palace, experienced in their own way, concurred that the substance baffled them as well. The princess, laid out in the banquet hall in which the couple was to celebrate their union (carried across its threshold by her new husband, a gesture so visibly romantic that I emulated it at my subsequent weddings, and now thanks to my example it is a tradition in several countries, though modern grooms forbear from weeping), was quite obviously expired and could not be revived by any touch, sound, or scent. And yet her heart would occasionally manage one soft beat, and a mirror held to her exquisite lips would, after several minutes, film over, however briefly, with a faint breath of life.

Gladdened as I and others were to observe that the princess had not entirely passed through the gates of death, this situation in its way was even crueler, for it filled our breasts with the intoxication of hope—and hope's torment. Equally tantalizing was the belief that Her Most Noble Grace would divulge the antidote, or at least the poison's name, that the authorities might furnish a cure. The duchess, however, continued to insist to her increasingly skeptical listeners that she had played no role in this intrigue. When at one point her son fell to his knees imploring his mother's help, she berated him in the harshest tones for his histrionics—a response, as I could have warned her if only she had sought my counsel, that blackened her further to the populace, and the emperor.

For many hours the premier minds of the duchy toiled to revive the princess, while I comforted her grieving grandmother, who sat with tears on her cheeks, stroking Wisdom's hand. Only when leeches were produced did Queen Benevolence suspend her mourning long enough to defend her granddaughter's tender flesh from those vampiric invertebrates and the equally vampiric physicians so ghoulishly wielding them. The banquet, laid out in anticipation of a reception that never came to pass, remained untouched on tables adorned with candles and white linens, the ice sculptures melting, the canapés cooling on their heavy silver platters—I reflect in particular on a savory meat pie flavored with raisins and honey that is apparently a great favorite in Montagne, which I can readily understand, as it was absolutely delicious—in fact irresistible.

At last, with many expressions of gratitude at my especial solicitation, the grieving old queen and and her equally grieving grandson-in-law sent us all away, requesting that they be afforded some privacy with the lifeless girl. The duke in fact declared that he himself would sleep in the banquet hall with a troop of his guards, that his bride not lie alone.

Weeping, he kissed her, and for a moment my hope rekindled that his kiss would revive her, as it does in so many children's tales. Oh, woe: it did not. The emperor, too, kissed her in his grandfatherly manner, to no avail. And so each of us went our own sad way, the room emptying into darkness. A day that had begun with such promise concluded with consummate tragedy, for I returned to my private tent to find a note from Tomas resting upon my silk pillow: "Ive heard the news + cannot bear it. Goodbye." My ward—my companion—my brilliant protégé—was gone.

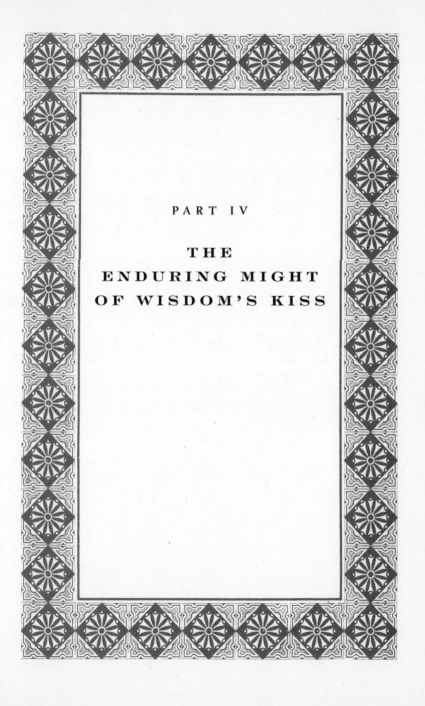

PART IV

THE
ENDURING MIGHT
OF WISDOM'S KISS

FROM THE DESK
of the
QUEEN MOTHER OF MONTAGNE,
& HER CAT

My Dearest Temperance, Queen of Montagne,

Oh, Granddaughter, I sit here a prisoner awaiting a verdict, not knowing if I will live or die — nor Dizzy, either!

I know you cannot better our crisis — indeed, I have little faith that these pages will ever reach your desk — yet I must do <u>something,</u> and transcribing the events of these past hours keeps my hands busy, and my mind somewhat preserved from madness.

My last missive, I believe, culminated with our most miserable discovery of the plot against Montagne. I had just sent your letter to the morning post when came a knock to our window: the acrobat Tips, returned at last from the duchess's balcony. He accepted Dizzy's efforts to remove the chill from his bones as I paced, so flummoxed I paid their embrace no heed.

"I could make a Doppelschläferin," Dizzy proffered at one point. Can you imagine? To mention witchcraft, particularly in the presence of one so close to the emperor! Her indiscretion was bested only by her illogic, for how in the world could an insensible double of Princess Wisdom ease the threat of your abdication, or Roger's claim to our throne? If anything, her unconsciousness would strengthen the case for his crowning!

I glared at her, hoping my fury would still her tongue. But too late, for the young man at once seized upon her utterance, saying it quite sounded like magic. Hastily I assured him it was not, causing the lad to chuckle. "Of course not! There's no such thing as magic. Not in Froglock or Bacio or anywhere."

"Nowhere?" your sister asked thoughtfully, as if it were the two of us alone . . . then without warning, leapt into the air, overcome by a sudden and mysterious epiphany. Straightaway she seized the lad and demanded to be taken to the emperor! Well! The emperor — so I retorted — had far better pursuits at this hour, not least of which was sleep, and I most certainly did not intend to traipse about Phraugheloch like a burglar.

Absorbing her fervor and mine, however, the young man extricated himself from Dizzy's grip, hurled himself out the window, and dashed off—down a ledge no wider than my two hands!

At once I turned on Dizzy. How dare she endanger herself and me and all our country by bandying words that could get us burnt simply by speaking them aloud! She hadn't the wit of Escoffier (who, wisely enough, slept through this) and frankly deserved to be bound to Duke Roger, as she was as stupid as he! Why should I waste my energy ensuring her safety when our kingdom would be far better served by my return to Montagne, where I would at least be heeded!

I might as well have shrieked at the wall, for your sister paid me not the slightest note, instead emptying every drawer and closet in the suite like a madwoman. When once I cornered and shook her, she only shook me in return: "Don't you see? Isn't it obvious?" No, dear Teddy, it was not. She then continued her frantic excavations.

At that point, quite at the height of my raging, the door of our suite cracked silently open and young Tips slipped in, accompanied most incongruously by an elderly laborer—a kindler, to be exact, complete with basket of twigs to lay the morning fire! Why in heaven's name either of them thought that we desired warming in the midst of this burning tragedy . . . then, hearing Dizzy's gasp, I studied anew the old man outfitted in the drab rags of a backstairs domestic, and gasped myself. This was no minion: it was Rüdiger IV, disguised to pass the halls at will!

Little time did I have to absorb this realization, however, before the <u>servant</u> straightened, and with a most <u>unservile</u> air demanded an explanation. Curtseying, Dizzy proffered him the scrap from the Globe d'Or, whispering to herself, "If this burns, then so shall we." Too late I realized her intent, and with a cry of dismay leapt toward her . . . as she with a word and a gesture performed the Spell of Elemental Fire.

Immediately flame appeared — dazzling, lapping and flickering, illuminating all the room — cupped in her two hands within the golden cloth, which held the searing fire without mark or stain. We all of us froze as if under enchantment, mesmerized by this spectacle, and myself at least by terror. Slowly the emperor stepped toward your sister, and slowly he reached toward the blaze — though not slowly enough, for his hand jerked back, and he stuck his finger into his mouth. Dizzy at once crumpled the fabric, snuffing the flame. He ordered her repeat her trick, which she did — then commanded she demonstrate whatever other witchery she might know!

Scrupulously avoiding my horrified eye, Dizzy sped through Elemental Air, producing a breeze that lifted the flame-filled cloth. "More," he directed, Tips gasping and marveling at this wonder. Dizzy murmured anew, and the golden cloth bearing its implausible freight of fire rose further into the air. Buoyed by the current emanating from her spread hands, the vessel floated high about the room, the flame's heat scorching the ghastly pink cherubs painted upon the ceiling.

The emperor turned to me, his face unreadable. He had not yet — I reassured myself — screamed for guards and executioners; perhaps we might escape this together, unscathed . . . but no. For at that moment — as baldly as though my granddaughter were a piece of meat or a flowerpot! — he informed me that he was "claiming this child for circus and empire" (again those dreadful words!) and demanded to know what compensation I wished in return — implying that his generosity in this regard should be swiftly and fervently acknowledged.

Panicked and appalled, terrified for your sister's life, I was unable even to conceive of a response to this cold-blooded monster, but could only collapse, overcome, onto a divan.

Dizzy on the other hand, who by this point was smiling so triumphantly that I feared her face would split in twain, turned to the man and in a most docile and obliging tone responded that Montagne wanted very little: only peace and sovereignty, forever.

Thank goodness I was already seated or I might have fainted outright! The emperor, however, did not flinch. "We should all of us like to see Farina's feathers cut. I had never imagined 'twould be Montagne wielding the shears, but it might work . . ."

The three of them huddle now plotting, too cautious even to call for water for fear the Phraugheloch staff might learn of their conclave. I would recount their whispers, but the triad refashions their grand plan by the minute. I have been declared too <u>morbid</u> — that is, too <u>practical</u> — to participate in their strategizing; I can only scribble to you.

Granddaughter, never in my life have I so begged the heavens that my words be read! Dizzy vows she will do everything in her power to see this letter delivered. If you do not receive these pages, it can mean only one thing: your sister has died in service to her country, and you and I and all of Montagne — or what is left of Montagne — shall be left to mourn her passing. Gracious, now I am weeping.

Emperor Rüdiger informs us that our suspicions of the mail service are well founded; it is probable that Wilhelmina's tentacles extend into every mail sack, and that you have not been sent any of my letters — and so have no knowledge of the nefarious scheme hatched against our kingdom! It is terrible, my dear — it breaks my heart to report it — but your charming suitor is no more than a poison-tongued viper sent to wheedle you off the throne and place Duke Roger in your stead! Your suitor's wickedness may extend even further, for we can only imagine the murderous lengths to which that hellcat Wilhelmina will go to acquire her family a royal title. Protect yourself, Granddaughter! Put your suitor under constant guard, preferably in a locked and windowless cell, until I return! Test your every mouthful for poison! Trust no one!

Oh, that our family might survive the days to come — you, with an entire kingdom to defend from infernal conspiracy; your sister, who in the next few hours shall face countless awful and unimaginable tribulations; myself, who through Escoffier shattered my vow against magic, a vow I made on pain of death, and I deserve no less than death for profaning it . . .

Pray for us all, Teddy! Pray hard!

Your terrified grandmother,
Ben

THE SUPREMELY PRIVATE DIARY
OF ~~WISDOM~~ *Dizzy* OF MONTAGNE

*Any Soul Who Contemplates Even Glancing
at the Pages of this Volume Will
~~Be Transformed into a Toad~~
Suffer a Most Excruciating Punishment.
On This You Have My Word.*

Saturday—afternoon—

We are reunited at last! 'Tis a miracle we have muddled our
way thus far—if I survive I shall never again complain about
anything & shall paint DO NOT COMPLAIN on the wall in
great letters to remind me of how v. bad life can get. Also to
remind myself of that moment last night (this morning? It was
either v. late or v. v. early) when he said <u>nowhere</u> but in a manner that inspired me to great thought about other countries &
Ambh & its Globe d'Or & at once I saw The Truth which has
never once before happened in my life that I can recall.

I was not certain however that it was The Truth nor were Tips and His Maj & we had no time whatsoever to test our theory as every subsequent moment was taken up with preparing for the wedding! Which I may state was horrible in every possible way! My gown was homely & ill-fitting & so uncomfortable— the Doppelschläferin is welcome to it. And the crowds were terrible—hordes of people goggling b/c they knew I was miserable & trapped—or b/c they were happy for Roger which is just as awful. Plus he spent the entire service whispering how his mother & I would be great friends—words he uttered with a straight face!

Altho thank goodness I didn't hear much I was so anxious while His Maj went on and on about ceremony & duty & who knows what else as I toiled to complete (in front of hundreds of people without anyone noticing!) the Doppelschläferin spell—that is almost complete it—& then hover with my body positively desperate to divide & then as His Maj told everyone to toss their hats right at that moment like a great bird diving for a fish—if that image works which I don't think it does—I grabbed this fish of opportunity & finished the spell & split into two bodies giving my <u>sleeping double</u> a jolly nudge right into Roger while I dove (like a bird!) under the curtain behind us. I'm afraid my D practically knocked him down—it was quite forceful more of a heave really than a nudge—but no one noticed they were all so busy retrieving their hats &

then Roger started making such a scene not to mention Nonna Ben wailing like a kettle—I hadn't realized how important it is that a queen know how to act—everyone chattering how the princess had been poisoned & you know who must have done it with the wine.

Imagine! None of us had even thought of pinning it on W! Which of course we wouldn't b/c we didn't know of that Farina marriage-toast tradition—I even tried not to drink it b/c Farina wine is usually terrible as it was today but thank goodness W is so bossy b/c now it's come back to ensnare her! Then I—the awake and hiding half of me that is and jolly glad I was to be awake & incognito—donned the old clothes we'd hidden & everyone was so busy gossiping they didn't even notice one little ragamuffin scurrying thru the streets of Froglock. And there he was waiting for me—just as we'd planned! So nervous because he had no idea if I was alive or dead—he'd heard I'd been poisoned & didn't know what to think—imagine his relief!

And his relief—our relief both which I can't even describe it was so intense—that I could actually operate the Globe d'Or! For once in my life a plan of mine actually succeeded! My Elemental Fire burns inside the sphere quite merrily from the sound of it—the Globe as energized as a horse tugging its bit which again isn't the best analogy but will have to do—it does respond to Elemental Air better than any horse I've ever had—perhaps I should try magic next time I ride that is if ever we reach ground b/c we are very high up which I am quite aware of from my perch on the Sultan's Throne—tho imagine fancying a sultan would sit here! The seat is so flimsy it's clearly for wizards and only stouthearted wizards at that—I may be the power driving this great hulking balloon but frankly I feel much more like the tail of a kite!

The G. d'O. now makes so much sense once one realizes that it requires <u>magic</u> to operate—it's a wonderful image really the sultan tooting about the skies with his consorts all reclining on pillows as their wizard or magus or jinn or whatever it is they have in Ahmb sitting on the <u>Sultan's Throne</u> and with Fire and Air serving as engine and pilot both. Tho landing presents a bit of a puzzle . . . Well we shall cross that bridge or whatever it is one crosses by air when the time comes. We have managed thus far have we not? Yes this is a severely mad misadventure but a grand one because I am still alive!!!

So now life would be utterly perfect were it not for one small yet critical detail—a side trip he has insisted we make & that I have no choice but to accept . . .

A Life Unforeseen
The Story of Fortitude of Bacio, Commonly Known as Trudy, as Told to Her Daughter

Privately Printed and Circulated

SHE WAS SO CLOSE! She had to escape! Desperately Trudy fought—her very life depended on it!—beating against the man grasping her so tightly. Yet strong arms pinned her hard, and twist as she might, she could not locate a shin to kick.

"Stop struggling, or we'll both fall!" hissed a familiar voice.

Yes, it was true—they were not falling—not yet, anyway. Instead of a face full of mud, Trudy found herself—most bafflingly!—rising up! Through the air! The wind redoubled, rippling Trudy's hair, and to her utter, lifelong amazement she found herself looking straight into the face of none other than her beloved Tips, who held her in his strapping grip as they rose, inexplicably, into the clouds.

A moment later, stupefied and gasping, Trudy found herself standing in the elegant rattan basket of the Globe d'Or. Tendrils of mist—no, *clouds!*—swirled about the basket's ropes, while far below, curled between the trees like an illustration in an atlas, was the road she had so recently trod; in the distance she could yet see the tavern and its yard, doll-size now, and a distant river looping through the pines.

Trudy gaped as Tips sealed the trapdoor in the basket's bottom and stowed the block and tackle that had hauled them so smoothly skyward—a machine operated, she noticed with dismay, by none other than Wisdom. Not even tattered clothes could disguise the princess, who with cool efficiency coiled a spool of cable, never taking her eyes from a compass set in the basket's rail.

"But—" began Trudy, "but you were poisoned!"

Wisdom shrugged. "So they say."

"But—" began Trudy again, turning to Tips, "but I did not *see* you!"

"You were headed for the hilltop right enough. Which is just what I needed, because the cable wouldn't reach the valley. And your hair was like a signal fire." He smiled at Trudy, but his smile held pain as well, and regret.

"She wasn't supposed to see us," the princess said under her breath. "That's why we stayed in the clouds."

"It's not the balloon she didn't see; it's me. Trudy can—how would you say it? She can see the future."

Trudy stared at Tips: that was a secret! One they had sworn to each other never to share, *ever*—and certainly not with Her Royal Dizzyness!

Her Highness, however, did not react in the slightest, but

simply scooped up the compass and shinned out of the basket onto an arrangement of wires and rods that didn't look sturdy enough to support a pigeon. With no apparent thought to the vast distance between herself and the ground far below, she settled herself onto a bit of bench and with a flourish spun backward and held out her hands, palms away. She was—most definitely—showing off.

Tips approached Trudy, stroking her arm. "Please . . . You've got magic, she's got magic—we're all in this together."

Trudy shot a suspicious look toward the princess, who with her back yet to them both cocked one arm, snapped her fingers, and produced a great handful of flame.

Trudy gasped. The princess made fire! Magically! And didn't even appear burnt by it!

Tips leaned toward Trudy. "Do you notice that we're sailing *into* the wind? Dizzy's creating air—wind—with her hands. She's blowing us east."

Trudy could now discern the approaching trees bent toward them, and the mist that in violation of every law of nature swirled against and not with the gliding Globe d'Or. "Oh . . . Can she do anything else?"

The princess turned to them at last. "*She* can also make water so we don't die of thirst up here, as we jolly well can't drink from clouds, and earth so . . . Oh! That's it! I'll make great heavy rocks so we can land!"

Trudy couldn't restrain herself. "You mean that you don't know how to land this thing? What—"

"I can land it *now*," the princess sniffed. "And what about you? You can see the future? Is that why you always looked like I was about to slap you?"

Trudy nodded. Her vision had come true: Wisdom *had* hurt her. She and Tips had hurt Trudy terribly, and now all that was left was the ache in her heart.

Trudy began to cry.

"Well. I need to . . . check things." So saying, the princess cranked her contraption up to the skin of the Globe d'Or and the rope ladder hanging from it and climbed the great sphere into the clouds.

Anxiously Tips watched Wisdom ascend, and with equal anxiety he turned back to Trudy.

"You—you—but you love *me!*" Trudy stepped toward him—then jumped at the hiss.

"Forgot to warn you—we've got Escoffier with us," Tips explained unnecessarily as the cat glowered.

"Glorious." Trudy, sobbing, collapsed onto the floor.

Lashing his tail most expressively, Escoffier climbed into her lap, his hot rough tongue licking the tears that ran down her arms.

Tips stared at her miserably. "I'm so sorry. I didn't mean to hurt you—I always thought I loved you. I *still* love you."

Trudy had dignity enough to snort.

"I do! I'll always love you. You're my family!"

"No, I'm not!" Trudy wailed. "I'm nobody's family. Don't you see? You have your brothers even if they're awful, and that little man, and now you've got *her,* but I have no one at all. It's a huge big world out there, and there's no one in it for me!" Too overcome to speak further, she buried her face in Escoffier and cried.

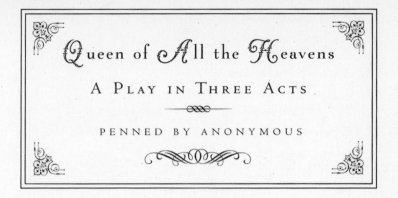

Act II, Scene iii.
The Globe d'Or.

Wisdom sits atop the Globe. Tips joins her.

TIPS: 'Tis dangerous, this globe, and taxing. I scale it daily, and I am winded.

WISDOM: I have no fear.

TIPS: Brave does not mean safe, my love. Please, don this belt—I wear its mate. Attached to this cable, you may prance about at will. Secure your feet here: you can now withstand a tempest.

WISDOM: How brilliant. With my Elemental Air I shall pilot our craft through the skies.

TIPS: You are as an angel! . . . But an angel bereft of jubilation.

WISDOM: O Tips! How could I celebrate when another sobs with broken heart?

TIPS: The same pain fills me. Trudy is my oldest, dearest friend; yet I have hurt her dreadfully.

WISDOM: If I had known . . .

TIPS: Would you have stopped? I did know and yet could not. For though she is my dearest friend, she is not my true love. That title belongs to another . . .

They embrace.

TIPS: The sky darkens. We should land, my darling, ere night falls.

WISDOM: No! Even now, Farina schemes against my home. Though I have hurt one girl, I may yet save another. Heaven knows it is the very least recompense I could make to my sister.

TIPS: You would travel through the night? 'Tis some kind of madness!

WISDOM: There is no sane alternative. If I weary, I need only imagine Roger—and his harpy mother!—claiming Montagne. Such nightmarish spectacle shall arouse me at once!

TIPS: Caution, my love. In your ire, you resemble a beautiful raptor poised for attack.

WISDOM: Then you are wise beyond measure to moor me to this Globe! No, vengeance waits until my sister, and her throne, are safe.

TIPS: And Trudy, too.

WISDOM: Yes, and Trudy, too. She deserves that, and happiness in abundance.

TIPS: Let us hope it comes to pass, for there is no truer friend in all the world than Trudy.

WISDOM: Well phrased, my love; and she has no truer friend than you.

They embrace.

A Life Unforeseen

The Story of Fortitude of Bacio, Commonly Known as Trudy, as Told to Her Daughter

Privately Printed and Circulated

RUDY BEGAN WEEPING even before she awoke the next morning. It took her several minutes, in fact, to reassure herself she *was* awake, so close to dream-state did this world appear: impenetrable white extending to infinity; a ceiling of gold above her head; Escoffier blithely cleaning his whiskers. And, only an arm's reach away, Tips asleep . . . with Wisdom asleep beside him, her head in his lap.

No, this was not a nightmare; it was an ever-worsening reality. Not only had she lost Tips, but she was now forced to occupy this wretched bucket of a conveyance as nothing more than a pointless and miserable addendum. The princess would not even land to let her off—if even the princess could, about which Trudy had more than a few doubts—for she was apparently in a "dreadful hurry." Instead Trudy was trapped in the worst possible place in the world.

Searching for a handkerchief to sop her streaming eyes, she found a scrap of paper tucked into her pocket. She opened it suspiciously, recognizing too well the heavy white vellum (ridiculously pretentious, Trudy had always thought, not that Tips was in any way responsible for his master's letterhead). Her suspicions proved correct, for it was a letter from Tips, written—so she learned from the first sentence—while he had sat outside the duchess's chambers in Phraugheloch. His words, true as they were—no, because of how true they were—cut her to the quick. He described himself as kin. Well, she didn't want kin! She wanted a lover—a mate—a husband! She sobbed in anger and despair.

"What is it?" Tips whispered from the bench opposite. He eased away from Wisdom to settle beside her. Escoffier sat, one paw midair, observing.

Trudy pulled away. "I don't want to be your family! I want to be your wife."

Gently Tips shook his head. "We haven't talked in six years. Everything you think—it's your thoughts, it's what you imagine. But it's nothing to do with me. This is my life, here—"

Across the basket, Wisdom shifted . . . opened her eyes—and hurled herself to her feet. "Where are we? This fog—I can't see a thing! Why didn't you wake me? Where's the compass?. . . Why are you both just sitting there?"

"It doesn't matter," Trudy said bitterly.

Tips, overcome, stared at the floor.

"*Doesn't matter?* It's the future of Montagne! It's *my* future, my sister's, it's——"

Trudy glared at her. "It's what? It's *my* future too? No, it's not. My future is over. You stole my future."

Wisdom recoiled. "How dare you!"

"How dare I? What's that, princess talk? How dare *you!* You can have anything you want, in the whole world. Why did you have to take him?"

Wisdom opened her mouth. She closed it again. "I'm sorry," she said at last. "I didn't 'take' him. I love him . . ."

"I hope we crash into a mountain! That's what your future should be!" Trudy glared at the princess and spun to glare at Tips——

Then froze. A beam, powerful as a lighthouse, flashed through the basket's weaving.

"Trudy?" Hesitantly Tips broke the silence. "What is it?"

Trudy rose to her feet, Escoffier joining her at the rail. She peered into the clouds. "Do you see that?"

Tips and Wisdom glanced at each other and shook their heads.

Now Trudy could see clearly. It was not a lighthouse, or a sunbeam——not natural light. It was joy. Shining out of the clouds was a promise of joy as powerful as anything she had ever known. She pointed with one quavering finger. "It's . . . happiness. That way." She turned to the others. "What's in that direction?"

"Montagne, of course," Wisdom answered promptly.

Trudy and Tips looked at her, baffled, and shared a baffled look between them.

Wisdom scowled. "What else would it be? Oh, please, don't be so obtuse. It's patently obvious . . . Isn't it?"

THE SUPREMELY PRIVATE DIARY
of ~~WISDOM~~ *Dizzy* of MONTAGNE

Any Soul Who Contemplates Even Glancing

at the Pages of this Volume Will

~~*Be Transformed into a Toad*~~

Suffer a Most Excruciating Punishment.

On This You Have My Word.

Sunday—morning—

I fell asleep! I don't believe it! Tips & I stood watch—we talked & talked atop the Globe avoiding the basket & that girl so miserable—she had Escoffier for company anyway. But then we did return & we fell asleep even tho we v. much didn't mean to & when I woke up we were in the middle of a great enormous impenetrable cloud completely lost & making matters so much worse Trudy was chastising Tips for the way he'd treated her being quite sharp which is v. unlike her & saying a great many things to him and to me too about which she clearly felt v. strongly—

But then she stopped & peered off into the clouds & said she saw happiness which I should quite like to know what that looks like but it was not the time to ask so instead I pointed out—because the two of them together were acting as dim as a box of rocks—that given that she was returning to Montagne it would make sense for her to be happy.

She & Tips looked at each other & she said she wasn't from Montagne. Which is completely stupid because of course she is! Why else would she have that ridiculous name—which I doubtless could have phrased more tactfully but it's not as if mine's any better. Wisdom? Temperance? Providence? These aren't names—they're not even decent virtues! A good virtue is being able to fly or to write thank-you notes in your sleep or something like that. At least Fortitude is something I would appreciate possessing particularly given how regularly I betray the name I bear now.

So I said that even tho she might not be from Montagne her mother must have been and I asked what *her* name was and Trudy said as if winning an argument that it was Mina. "Which is short for . . . ?" I asked. Because everyone I know with a name so pretty & short has a real name behind it that's ugly & long. Then Trudy thought for a moment & then whispered because you could tell she was only just remembering that her mother's real name was Mindwell. Which is extremely ugly & extremely virtuous & only someone from Montagne would ever inflict something that awful on a poor defenseless little baby girl!

Which I said—altho somewhat better than that I hope—& Trudy thought for a long while & then nodded so you'd think she was agreeing to wage war & she looked into the cloud & pointed.

If she is wrong we will crash into a mountain & die. But I don't think she is.

I'm v. pleased that I apologized to her about Tips. She deserves it.

THE IMPERIAL ENCYCLOPEDIA
OF LAX

8TH EDITION

Printed in the Capital City of Rigorus
by Hazelnut & Filbert, Publishers to the Crown

MONTAGNE, CHATEAU DE

Situated at the mouth of the great fertile valley of Montagne, overlooking the switchbacked road that constitutes the valley's only point of entry, Chateau de Montagne has for centuries been the best-defended fortification in the empire, and possibly its most attractive. As the Kingdom of Montagne has historically been linked to sorcery, so, too, was its royal seat, and for many generations men whispered of magical passageways secreted within the chateau walls. The chateau's roofs and parapets, framed against the mountain of Ancienne and culminating in the high "Wizard Tower," present a most arresting spectacle. Within the chateau, the inner courtyard displays a neoclassical symmetry utterly devoid of repetitiousness or pedantry. Of particular note, and open to the public on state holidays, are the Great Hall; the Hall of Flags; the Throne Room; the Ballroom, paved in rose and ebon marble; and the Solstice Terrace. Recently erected on the north face of the chateau, the terrace projects over the high cliffs that define and protect the Montagne valley. Though most definitely to be avoided by acrophobics, the terrace provides an unmatched vista of the western mountains, particularly at sunset.

A Life Unforeseen

The Story of Fortitude of Bacio, Commonly Known as Trudy,
as Told to Her Daughter

Privately Printed and Circulated

INDWELL! Trudy had not thought of that
name in twelve years!

It was wondrous, in fact, that she recalled it at all. Trudy
could not have been more than five when she overheard a conversation between her mother and a handsome traveler as the
Duke's Arms wound down for the night. Where are you from,
the man asked, because your accent is not of Alpsburg. Normally
Mina ignored such questions with a shrug, but this night she
only laughed and replied, "My true name is Mindwell and that
is answer enough."

Trudy's young mind could not fathom such a name, and
Tips when she told him replied she must have dreamt it. And so
Trudy agreed she had, and believed it until this moment. But it
had been no dream. Her mother had been named for a virtue.
Her mother—who had promised to tell her someday of her

heritage but died before that promise could be fulfilled—her mother had come from Montagne.

Tips nodded. He had not forgotten Mindwell either.

Now Trudy stood in the basket of the Globe d'Or, pointing one shaking finger into the cloud that engulfed them—staring until her eyes ached and tears streamed down her face—and announced, "That way."

Escoffier pressed his warm body against her as he, too, peered into the blankness. Tips stood on her other side, though Trudy was far too preoccupied to concern herself with him, or Wisdom. She had more important concerns, for the vision of joy shining from those impenetrable clouds drew her with the same relentless power that draws the magnet north.

Escoffier began to mew, his tail lashing. Yet Trudy could see nothing in that oppressive white mist . . . and then she could. "Look!"

A post loomed out of the cloud. No, not a post. An iron spire, attached to a steep conical roof sheathed in tile.

"It's a tower!" exclaimed Wisdom. "Good heavens, it's the Wizard Tower, of our chateau!" She could not resist a hug—though only a brief one—to Trudy. "You're brilliant! Now we can rescue Teddy, and Montagne!"

The cone shape slowly materialized . . . revealing a platform carved into the slope as a pier is carved into seafront stones, edged with heavy iron rings.

"It's a dock!" Tips clapped Wisdom on the back. "How clever!"

Instead of elation, however, the princess blanched, her face clouding with something close to fear. "I've . . . I've never seen that before. The Wizard Tower is—well, just be careful, will you? It's not—it's not human."

"Of course it's not; it's a tower." But Tips's fingers strayed to check the buckle of his sword belt, and he could not resist an anxious glance at Trudy.

She smiled back at him, beneficent in her newfound authority. To her, the tower radiated only peace. "It's fine."

So reassured, Tips leapt out as the basket scraped against the platform's slate pavers, helping Trudy (how nice it felt, his hands on her waist, however briefly!) and securing the balloon to the great iron rings.

Instinctively—for the tower, she could see, was *expecting* her—Trudy reached for a small door tucked into the platform wall, and before Wisdom could do more than strangle out a warning, she drew it open. Escoffier at once dashed into the dimness. With a reassuring glance at Trudy, Tips followed. Wisdom, on the other hand, kept a tight grip on the basket rail, testing the slate pavers against her weight. She smiled grimly at Trudy, then entered.

Marveling at her burgeoning confidence, Trudy ducked through the dark doorway herself. Almost at once she stumbled upon a spiral staircase, each step no wider than she was. She could barely make out a room—or roomlet, really—spread below her in the gloom. Vague shadows shifted in the corners as she descended.

Wisdom stood in the roomlet's center, staring at the spiral staircase as though she'd never seen it before. "I've never seen this before," she whispered hoarsely. "And I've been up here hundreds of times. Thousands . . ."

"It keeps going, you know." Tips stood, Escoffier mewing around his ankles, studying a hole in the floor: the spiral staircase continuing downward.

Wisdom slipped to Trudy's side. "Is this safe?" she whispered. "Because there's another staircase over there, a real one, that's the one we're supposed to use—that's the one I always use, and I know exactly where I end up—I mean, I've always known up to now, anyway—I'm babbling, aren't I? But that hole doesn't look safe to me."

Trudy, mesmerized, moved toward the darkness. "We have to go down there."

Wisdom again shuddered and then, belatedly remembering her position, declared that she should lead; it was her castle, after all. With a flourish and a mutter, she produced a bright handful of flame that sent the shadows flickering.

And so, princess at the fore, they descended.

The descent lasted hours—no, that was impossible. It could not have been more than ten minutes, but in that sepulchral darkness it felt interminable, the dust and damp melded into a slime that coated the impossibly narrow treads, the rough walls abrading Trudy's skirt and fingertips, the incessant and nauseating turning . . . and always the throbbing insistence, shining from the depths, that they *hurry*.

"Found it!" Wisdom called out at last, though "it" would have been quite difficult not to find: a wide, crude door with a latch fashioned from a shovel. Tips—who, Trudy now recalled, had always been a bit claustrophobic—at once pulled the door open a crack and breathed a sigh of relief at the daylight that seeped in. They all jockeyed to see, Escoffier worming his way between their legs.

"Where are we?" Tips whispered.

Wisdom snorted. "Of course! The gardening sheds. That's where she always is—she likes *plants*." Stating this as if the concept were absolutely inconceivable.

Hurry, hurry, yes—but where, exactly? Peering past Tips's elbow, Trudy observed a courtyard cluttered with flowerpots and wheelbarrows and great mounds of dirt; a greenhouse filled one wall. In the distance several men repotted flowers as a farmer led a horse and wagon.

"I can't go out there," Wisdom continued. "If word spreads that I was seen in Montagne when I'm supposed to be in Farina practically dead . . . Besides, *she* never listens to me anyway."

I can't imagine why not, Trudy thought. She felt a pang of sympathy for this Temperance person; life could not be easy with a sister like Wisdom. Trudy peered out again past the clutter of rakes and shovels, examining the gardeners, the greenhouse—

A blast of emotion struck her, so powerful that she staggered back.

Tips caught her elbow. "What is it?"

"Something—someone—greenhouse—" Trudy gasped, overwhelmed by the sensation of crisis and by the imperative need for haste.

Wisdom yanked open the door. "Go!" She pushed Tips, then Trudy, through the opening. *"Save her!"*

MEMOIRS
OF THE
MASTER SWORDSMAN
FELIS EL GATO

Impresario Extraordinaire ✦ Soldier of Fortune
Mercenary of Stage & Empire

LORD OF THE LEGENDARY
FIST OF GOD

Famed Throughout the Courts and Countries of the World

&

The Great Sultanate

✻ THE BOOTED MAESTRO ✻

WRITTEN IN HIS OWN HAND ~ ALL TRUTHS VERIFIED ~ ALL BOASTS REAL

A Most Marvelous Entertainment,
Not to Be Missed!

THE TRAGIC INCAPACITATION of the winsome Princess Wisdom—less than a day after Her Highness, to our most mutual satisfaction, had made my acquaintance—was a heartbreak not just to me, the duchy, and all the empire, but especially to poor Tomas, who was altogether destroyed by this crushing news. Departing his quarters in extreme wretched-ness, he stumbled upon the Globe d'Or moored and lonesome in a field, forgotten in the tumult of tragedy. Despondently he climbed aboard (so he later reported to me), only to find the vessel occupied already by an impoverished lass seeking shelter from the lowering clouds, a lass who as it happened bore an uncanny resemblance to the poisoned princess. Perhaps it was this that caught the lad's attention, for soon he found himself conversing with the girl so intently that neither noticed the loosening of my well-tied knots, and the balloon floating, un-manned and without power (for *someone*, a miscreant whom I have never been able to identify, had removed the charcoal and the brazier!), into the heavens. So high were they when finally they realized their terrifying predicament that their shouts did not reach earth, and the two huddled in each other's arms, their fate in the sway of the pitiless elements, the wind taking them they knew not where.

I must pause here to clarify one matter, for rumors have circulated for decades that this maid, bearing the dull but respectable name of Violet la Riene, was none other than Princess Wisdom traveling incognito. This—as I more than anyone in the empire should know—is patently impossible. Her Highness had the pleasure of my company on two occa-sions, once for several hours, and Violet la Riene flourished for many years under my brilliant tutelage; I better than anyone can assert that the two young women were as different as is day from night. The princess had a radiance unmatched by any commoner. She spoke with grace, sweetening her words with noble gestures and kindly sentiments, in a manner that Violet la Riene, much as I enjoy the girl, could never hope to match. Indeed, Mademoiselle la Riene at times spouted a vocabulary more suited to sailors than lasses, words that would never soil the lips of a princess. The two differed in height, coloring, and the placement of moles. I concede that Mademoiselle la Riene's skill upon the stage, and her magnetic effect upon every audience before which she appeared, were quite reminiscent of Princess Wisdom, but that should be ascribed wholly to my skilled instruction and my ability to transfer the inspiration with which Princess Wisdom had filled me into another adept performer.

At that moment, however, trapped in that vessel of doom, the two could not possibly perceive the future success of Violet, or of Tomas, paired with her in the ring and out. Instead they sailed through the heavens—so they described to me later, with understandable pain—in the belief that every breath would be their last, for if the Globe d'Or did not crash to earth, killing them instantly, it would doubtless impale itself on a tree or mountainside, leaving them broken, slowly to perish of exposure. At one point Tomas, peering over the side, recognized the red locks of that ubiquitous Trudy, and tossed her a rope, that she might draw them to safety. Lamentably, the boy's good intent surpassed his reason, for the powerful sphere lifted the tavern wench at once, giving her no recourse but to join the duo in the basket.

How they survived the terrors of that night I cannot imagine. Oh, the thirst! The hunger! The dark! The winged nocturnal predators seeking out their tender young flesh! Yet survive they did, and by the enigmatic hand of fate ended up marooned on the highest tower of the Chateau de Montagne. Alighting upon this famed castle, my ward Tomas learned that Temperance, queen of that fair kingdom, in a fit of despair was at that very moment abdicating the throne! This intelligence stirred every fiber within Tomas's manly heart, for well he recognized the desperate deeds that sometimes accompany loss of hope. The Globe d'Or had traveled so speedily that no word had yet arrived of the tragedy of Wisdom's Kiss; Tomas alone knew that with the princess stricken, the kingdom would be without heir and so pass to Roger. Fond as Tomas might be of the duke—and the lad through my wise counsel held the empire's nobility in highest esteem—he justly felt that Temperance should be alerted to this most recent circumstance ere she committed to any immutable course of action.

He sprinted to the young woman's assistance, only to find her sequestered with a gardener, inscribing the final signature on the page that would seal her fate and the kingdom's. Even as Tips and Trudy approached—Violet having adjourned elsewhere—the gardener snatched up the document and hid it on his person. Readily displaying the poise I had instilled in him, Tomas requested its return and hastened to inform the queen of the true breadth of this drama. The gardener responded by drawing a hidden sword and demanding that Tomas step aside so he might return to his *real* mistress. At this the young queen burst into tears, for she had evidently expected her abdication to be followed by an elopement with her pandering companion. Tomas to his distress could not offer comfort, for the man—a scoundrel, and certainly no gardener—at that moment attacked, and the lad barely had time to draw his own weapon.

Wretchedly, at that very moment I myself was in Froglock occupied with a not-inconsiderable drama of my own, the resuscitation (failed, alas!) of poor Princess Wisdom. Therefore, in recounting this epic skirmish, I shall present myself as notional witness, basing my narrative on others' fervid descriptions.

Around the greenhouse the two men battled. Pots shattered, palms toppled, the queen sobbed and wailed as Trudy did her female best to tender comfort and keep her from distracting these warriors. One time the man had Tomas pinned to a wall, blade at his neck, but at this moment the cat Escoffier leapt into the face of the wretch and scratched him so viciously that the man staggered back, releasing Tomas from certain death.

The villain raced outside, Tomas on his heels crying, "He flees! He flees!" his shouts attracting a crowd. Though the other fought hard, Tomas had the advantage of youth and resilience, and redoubled his parries. The coward responded by mounting his waiting horse and making for the courtyard gate. My training once again proved its excellence, for Tomas followed, leaping from cart to wheelbarrow to an angled plank that launched him, somersaulting, through the air. With a cheer from the awestruck spectators, Tomas landed behind the man, dragged him from his mount, and, having relieved him of that most precious document, dashed away.

By ill luck, the mist lingering like smoke in every corner overwhelmed my ward's sense of direction, and too soon the lad found himself on a broad terrace without means of escape, the scoundrel at his heels demanding both the writ of abdication and the lad's head. The fight grew ever fiercer. Twice Tomas faced death, and twice evaded it through strength alone (which is precisely why my daily regimen of calisthenics is so essential to any performer). He yet clutched the parchment, now damp from perspiration and flecked with blood, but with every swing of their weapons, the other drew closer to victory. Pressed against the terrace balustrade, Tomas had no choice but to climb upon it; should he tumble, only clouds would slow his fall.

Gasping and panting, my protégé fought on, his opponent striking at his legs and feet, intent on maiming, then butchering, our warrior. Never before had Tomas's half decade of training with the empire's most skilled swordsman served him so well, for few men could labor when backed against such vast emptiness. Still, he weakened. Desperate for respite, Tomas put to use his sole remaining asset and with a taunting phrase held the paper over the misty void.

The adversary paused. As tremendously as the man wished Tomas slaughtered, he craved that document still more. He

leapt upon the balustrade and grasped Tomas with one powerful hand while with the other seizing that priceless sheet. The
two men grappled, swaying now over the gulf, now back, each
refusing to release. The breathless crowd drew near, spectators
pressed upon each other, yet no observer was foolhardy enough
to reach out, for any attempt at rescue could as easily result in
death. (If only I had been present to serve deliverance!) And
then—

With a cry of triumph Tomas ripped the paper from the
other's hand. The man roared in fury. Lunging at the lad, he
reached too far—lost his balance—and plunged backward
off the balustrade! Scrabbling at the air, he for a brief second
caught Tomas's jerkin—and in so doing dragged my apprentice
off the railing and into the void!

Their screams faded as the two men plunged into oblivion.
On the terrace, each viewer absorbed in stillness this horror,
the silence broken only by women's sobs. The brilliance of this
duel, the unparalleled drama against an awesome backdrop, the
last mist burning away to reveal that peerless vista of mountain
peaks bedecked in the luminous green of spring!

And then—a gasp! Rising like a vision before that shattered crowd was none other than Tomas, standing astride a
magnificent sphere of gold. In one hand he held the writ of
abdication, flames lapping it into ash; as he reached the level
of the balustrade, he—ever the well-coached showman!—with
a smile blew the blackened fragments to the crowd, then leapt
onto the terrace for a hero's welcome.

THE SUPREMELY PRIVATE DIARY
OF ~~WISDOM~~ *Dizzy* ~~,~~ OF MONTAGNE

Any Soul Who Contemplates Even Glancing

at the Pages of this Volume Will

~~Be Transformed into a Toad~~

Suffer a Most Excruciating Punishment.

On This You Have My Word.

Sunday—dusk—

O! To imagine I would ever pen these words: today was too exciting. 'Tis miraculous I can even hold a quill my hand shakes so!—yet I must record these events while still they dominate my consciousness—forevermore when some indicting louse sneers that I do not live up to my name I shall comfort myself that at least once in my life I acted wisely.

Trudy—(it's absolutely astounding by the way—she has no sense of how lovely she is! Can you imagine? The silly believes the whispers & stares that greet her appearance stem from cruelty! How v. stupid some people are!) (altho now that I dwell upon the matter I see the link 'twixt cruelty & envy—I must commit to improvement on that front)—led us straight to Chateau de Montagne—to the Wizard Tower!—which once again dumbfounded me by producing out of veritable thin air a spiral staircase that pierced the building as a knitting needle would a stack of books—or a layer cake perhaps—my analogy suffers but I have not time to make it right—needless to say we were delivered faster than a dropping rock to ground level where we found Temperance in her precious greenhouse even at that moment signing away Montagne.

I, of course, could not reveal myself—were word to slip out that the poisoned princess was frolicking in Montagne we would quite have to forfeit this game—& so was left dancing in frustration behind a door while Tips & Trudy—& Escoffier!—rushed to save her. O, I near lost my mind as I waited! And then out rushed a stranger—handsome enough tho with evil in his eyes—whatever was Teddy thinking in losing her heart to him?!—grasping a sword!—with Tips hot on his heels shouting, "He flees! He flees!"

Well! I could not but think that this was a message to me—which indeed it was Tips assured me later he is so v. clever—& straightaway I decided—particularly since I could make no contribution otherwise—that it was up to me to pursue that fleeing scoundrel.

Dashing back up the staircase I hurled myself aboard the G d'Or & cast off driving that great lumbering orb toward the cliff that I might from above observe the fiend's escape & mark him much as an eagle gliding on high marks its prey—an image I quite relish I must say—& thus guide our soldiers to this evildoer.

So it was that I hovered over the switchback highway that descends Montagne's great cliff. Yet no fiend appeared & while I scanned the earth seeking him out I heard shouts—Tips & the villain above me engaged in desperate battle! Hastily I scaled the orb that I might watch more closely & good it was I did so for the two men—grappling for a scrap of paper that could not but bode ill for my kingdom—at that very moment plunged off the platform to their doom!

Tips—how brave he is!—in falling aimed for the balloon while I tossed him a cable which saved him I think. The fiend fell on the other side his clawlike hands scratching at the balloon but he could make no purchase & with a scream of horror continued his descent after many awful seconds striking the ground far below. Splat. And good riddance to any man who treats my sister so. Tips on the other hand quite nimbly scaled the G d'Or—giving me a hasty kiss which I did not make a single attempt to spurn—& sent me back to the basket (tho I could not resist first setting alight that despicable parchment) that I might return him & myself unseen to the chateau.

Which I did & while hiding in the basket observed his hero's welcome tho he did not linger as every moment in that crowd increased the chances I would be revealed—& now we journey together without a chaperone! Which would make certain tongues wag I am sure yet we are both the soul of decorum for we are too exhausted to behave otherwise! Tips is understandably drained from his great battle & after a little nursing on my part (little being all the nursing of which I am capable) collapsed asleep—a condition in which I shall quite soon join him.

This has been such an extraordinary adventure—someday perhaps it might be possible to share it with the world—it would make a most remarkable novel or even a play—tho one would need great skill with a pen to manage that feat! But I cannot dwell upon storytelling at the moment—I am off to dreamland then anon to dazzle the empire (that is I hope I shall dazzle & not fall on my prat!) as Violet la Riene! (Is that not a brilliant pseudonym? Rien means "nothing" & reine means "queen"—a perfect description of me! And violet of course is a lovely flower and a lovely color too, but most importantly it is not a virtue. No one in the history of Montagne would ever say "Oh, Violet, for once can't you just behave violetly?")

O I am so happy I can scarcely bear it.

A Life Unforeseen

The Story of Fortitude of Bacio, Commonly Known as Trudy, as Told to Her Daughter

Privately Printed and Circulated

LATER, Trudy would endeavor to recall her first impressions of Queen Temperance, to separate them from the insight and appreciation that she in the ensuing years developed. To be sure, their first encounter in the greenhouse—Temperance hysterical from embarrassment and grief, Trudy terrified for Tips's life—was not the most auspicious. Yet even then Trudy could see past the passion and tumult to know that Tips would probably survive and that Temperance was a precious soul indeed. They clung to each other through that epic battle, Trudy murmuring words of comfort, and as they listened to the death scream of that odious Farina spy, she whispered, "He is gone . . . he is gone . . . he is gone," as though it were an invocation, or a prayer, and it was not clear which man it was she prayed for.

Wisdom, and Nonna Ben more obliquely, had described Temperance as timid and shy, but such was not the young

woman Trudy came to know. Even that first night, the young queen—while rightly cursing the duplicity of a man who would woo her with dogwoods—forbore from weeping over her own humiliation to query Trudy about Wisdom's wedding, the duchess's plot, and the whole of the Froglock experience. She had not received correspondence from Nonna Ben in four days and was desperate for the minutest scraps of information Trudy could provide. Escoffier sat with pricked ears as they puzzled out the chronology, so attentive that they could not but believe Nonna Ben was observing them through his eyes, and they took care to address the cat as if he *were* Ben, a courtesy to which he did not object in the least.

Together the two young women pored over Nonna Ben's latest missive (sent via the Globe d'Or and hand delivered by Trudy herself), describing Wisdom's display of magic to the emperor and his response, fragments of which Trudy had already heard aboard the balloon. Trudy listened in sympathetic horror as her new friend relayed the poisonous words that the duchess's agent had dripped in her ears, and she comforted her that no young woman could resist such sly manipulation. "It's perfectly shameful to tell someone you love her but she shouldn't be queen. If you truly loved someone, you'd tell the world she should be empress, even if she was only a featherbrained milkmaid! And someday someone will say that about you—although you're not a featherbrain, you know. Or a milkmaid."

Temperance laughed and said she knew *that* at least, and

Escoffier lounging between them waved his tail contentedly as he purred.

Trudy even explained her sight, which she had never discussed with another soul except her mother and Tips (and, on that one awful occasion, Wisdom). Yet she sensed—she saw— that the queen would appreciate it. Indeed the queen did, though not without first expressing chagrin that yet another person had magic while she had none, and pressing Trudy for details on Mindwell's heritage, details Trudy was unable to provide. So instead they discussed Tips and Wisdom, whether the two at that very moment might be floating through the vault of heaven, and what Ben must be up to in Froglock, though whatever it was—they reassured each other—she was doubtless safe as evinced by Escoffier's phlegmatic demeanor.

The mystery of Trudy's bloodline deepened the next morning when Temperance offered Trudy a tour and led her through the gardens and spaces of the magnificent Chateau de Montagne. Entering the Throne Room, Trudy without a moment of hesitation strode across the vast chamber to a humble old stool set in the shadows of the throne. Sitting herself upon it, she turned expectantly toward Temperance.

"What in heaven's name are you doing?" the queen asked, not without amusement.

"I—I'm sorry—" Trudy leapt up, blushing furiously. "It just came over me! I didn't—I'm so embarrassed . . ."

"Please, don't be! Do you know—well, how could you? That's the counselor's seat—the counselor to the throne. It's a terribly important position, and very few rulers are lucky enough—and you—oh, goodness! You went right over and plunked yourself—and with your sight—oh my, do you know what this means?"

Trudy could not answer, for her sight momentarily overwhelmed her, the joy matching in intensity the light that she'd observed from the Globe d'Or. She could see her own joy, yes, but the queen's as well, their two fates bound fast . . . Standing there, Trudy looked at the queen before her and at the same time saw the queen in years and decades to come, the room swirling with visitors and diplomats not yet arrived—not yet even born—all turning toward her, toward Trudy, seeking her counsel. Seeking her sight.

Trudy's mind spun. If she accepted this position, she could remain here in this lovely chateau forever. She need never return to Bacio.

The queen continued to stammer. "Do you think you might . . . want . . . it? The position, I mean. And the seat as well—they rather go together, you see . . ."

"Yes, I do see," Trudy answered as last with a radiant smile. "Yes. I do."

✦ ✦ ✦

That very afternoon, Trudy sent a letter to Eds informing him that, sadly, she would not be returning to the Duke's Arms, as she had accepted employment elsewhere; he must find himself a new kitchen wench. She included in the envelope a gold coin—her payment from Nonna Ben—knowing that currency was a language Eds spoke far better than words. Then she took up residence, with her bundle of clothes and earrings and Tips's letters, in a suite within Chateau de Montagne, counseling the queen whenever Temperance wished it. With time, the words "Lady Fortitude" did not make her wince, or glance behind her for the noblewoman to whom the other must be speaking. The queen assisted in this by declaring Trudy a peeress of the realm, complete with a gilded legal document that Trudy kept hidden in a drawer in her bedroom but admired sometimes at night, when she was certain no one could observe her.

Temperance unraveled as well the mystery of Trudy's lineage—unraveled it quite promptly, in fact, even before they had received the reassuring news that "Violet" and Tips had landed safely, if conspicuously, in the city of Rigorus, there awaiting the return of His Imperial Majesty and Circus Primus. Trudy this day was at her post in the Throne Room, doing her best to absorb the innumerable details and protocols of statecraft. A bearded gentleman entered bearing a parchment. Seeing him, Trudy found herself blind-sided with a swirl of emotions so powerful that she almost swooned.

Escoffier, settled in her lap, opened one and then both eyes to watch, though he did not deign to raise his head.

"Your Majesty." The bearded gentleman bowed to Temperance. "I have at last the information you seek. But it is"—here he glanced toward Trudy—"it is nuanced. Perhaps we could speak privately?"

No, they could not, returned the queen, for it was Trudy's duty and the queen's wish that she hear all, and moreover Lady Fortitude, if she should ever properly assist with Montagne's future, must without doubt learn her own past. And so the gentleman, with roundabout phrasing and unrolling of papers and as much consideration as he could muster, commenced to explain Lady Fortitude's genealogy.

His solicitude baffled Trudy, for she did not know this word *genealogy* . . . until she realized with a start that he meant her history. Her family.

Without warning, she began to cry. She would finally learn who she was, and Mina, and whence they hailed.

Temperance drew her close and offered a handkerchief, begging the gentleman to continue.

The story was a sad one (so the gentleman related), though in the main unexceptional: Lady Fortitude's mother—born and raised in Montagne, as her name suggested—was the lone child of a stern wool merchant, who on discovering her love for a lowly stone carver disowned her. Soon thereafter, the young man fell to his death, and Mina, obviously with child, fled Montagne forever. The wool merchant had since perished, as had the stone carver's parents, so Trudy to some extent was as orphaned as ever.

However—so the gentleman added—there was more to the tale. Mindwell's forebears had been wool merchants since the dawn of time, as stolid and unimaginative as the sheep who made their wealth. But the stone carver . . . Pierre Stein was his name, and he came from a long line of artisans and artists who by rumor, scandal, and at least once by marriage (here the bearded gentleman pointed to an ancient name on that sinuous genealogy) had been connected to the royal family. Pierre Stein's maternal grandmother could grow herbs even in the dead of winter, and a great-great-great-uncle had been famous for his ability to predict the weather, indeed in this capacity serving the then-king of Montagne.

"Oh," said Trudy, having no idea how to respond to this information.

"Thank you, sir," Temperance interjected smoothly. "As always, you are a credit to your profession; the anecdotes in particular we enjoyed immensely. Might you leave us this parchment to study privately?"

But of course; the document was now the property of Lady Fortitude. With a bow to them both, the gentleman withdrew.

Temperance bent over the paper, tracing the generations. "Reason . . . Beauregard . . . Giorgio . . . Compassion . . . Compassion was a witch, you know. An *amazing* witch, from what they say." She looked up at Trudy with shining eyes. "Her son—"

"If the rumors are correct," interjected Trudy, who had listened most closely to the bearded gentleman's presentation.

"Oh, pooh, rumors are always correct; he's just being polite. Do you see? Compassion's second son had a—well, you know—a love affair, with this woman here—Chastity. A lovely name, though not particularly apt in this situation. But it means that your great-something-something-something grandfather was of royal blood."

"Which," Trudy interjected, seeing Temperance's point at last, "explains my sight! It's the magic blood you're always talking about, that magic royal blood."

"Oh, it's more than that!" Temperance clutched Trudy's hand in delight. "Don't you see? You're my—I'm—we are and we'll always be . . . We're family!"

THE IMPERIAL ENCYCLOPEDIA
OF LAX

8TH EDITION

Printed in the Capital City of Rigorus
by Hazelnut & Filbert, Publishers to the Crown

FORTITUDE OF BACIO
(CONTINUED)

Arriving, however unconventionally, in Montagne, Fortitude quickly made the acquaintance of young Queen Temperance; the two distant cousins formed a bond that would last both their lives. Inexperienced and fearful, Temperance benefited immeasurably from Fortitude's companionship and appears to have truly believed in the other's clairvoyance. Nor was Queen Temperance alone in this regard; too soon the fallacy of Lady Fortitude's psychic powers spread throughout the populace, until every petitioner and diplomat approaching the queen found himself grappling with the nebulous and exasperating question of whether his words—indeed, his very appearance—would make Fortitude, and thus Temperance and all the subjects of Montagne, "happy." Thus the prophetess, however counterfeit, elicited an unprecedented constraint on warmongering and greed; peace flourished, and Temperance's rule came to be known as the Reign of Tranquility. Fortitude's family history may be found in *The Comprehensive Genealogical Encyclopedia of Montagne*. Though courted by many suitors, Lady Fortitude ultimately married Count Rudolph of Piccolo, a local landowner who, to honor their nuptials, grew a pumpkin so large that they rode inside it to the wedding ceremony. They had two daughters. Faith, the firstborn, married Temperance's son Henri, and as queen of Montagne counseled her husband as diligently as Fortitude had counseled his mother; Humor, the younger of the two, assisted Fortitude with her memoirs (published privately).

The Gentle Reflections
of Her Most Noble Grace,
Wilhelmina, Duchess of Farina,
within the Magnificent Phraugheloch Palace
in the City of Froglock

The world continues to believe me a murderess—but an incompetent one!

Oh! I am affronted!

Worse, His <u>Imperial Stupidity</u> considers mail theft a capital offense—and speaks so explicitly of the <u>crime</u> of stealing letters that it is almost as if he anticipated my disclosure and seeks to avert it!

(If stealing letters were truly a crime, I would be dead a thousand times over.)

Were I to reveal my <u>proof</u> that Queen Benevolence is a witch, I would be <u>arrested</u>!

That <u>sorceress</u> has him completely transfixed—at least Handsome has driven off her loathsome feline—it is one small comfort that I have inflicted <u>some</u> suffering on that hag of a queen.

Roger pays me no attention whatsoever—and his brother Hrothgar still does not write! Worse, my most brilliant agent—whom I planned to adopt as a <u>true</u> son!—is now dead.

Were it not for Handsome, I would be without companionship—yet my friend's amiable camaraderie is all I require—oh, treasured dog, would that you could rule when I am gone!

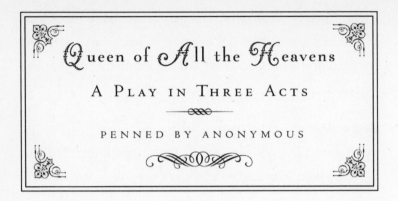

Queen of All the Heavens

A PLAY IN THREE ACTS

PENNED BY ANONYMOUS

Act II, Scene v.
Phraugheloch Palace Banquet Room.

Wisdom lies in a glass coffin.
Enter Rüdiger IV, Benevolence, Wilhelmina, Roger and attendants.

RÜDIGER: What gruesome draught it must have been to fell this
vibrant princess so.

BENEVOLENCE: A fortnight has passed, and still she neither lives
nor dies.

WILHELMINA: Your Majesty, I beg you hear me out: I had no hand
in this crime. I swear it.

BENEVOLENCE [*aside*]: 'Tis irony indeed that the vixen is penal-
ized for the one offense she did not perpetrate.

RÜDIGER: Your actions betray your words, Your Grace. Once before a poisoning was attempted on this innocent; this time, good

fortune failed her. My duke, tell me: will you obey your vows and attend your bride?

ROGER: The law would have that I attend her, but my heart cries out that I adore her. O my beloved, I shall be at your side forever!

BENEVOLENCE: Well phrased, well phrased indeed. [*Aside*] Farina, now bound to this lifeless form! Thus can no alliance be configured against Montagne.

RÜDIGER: None could ask for more devotion. And yet while Farina has gained a wife, Montagne is deprived of a daughter. Though murder has not transpired, a penalty must still be levied.

BENEVOLENCE [*aside*]: Now comes the unveiling of His Majesty's grand strategy!

RÜDIGER: Farina, we would you granted this grieving nation Alpsburg and Bridgeriver in recompense.

WILHELMINA: Two territories, so wealthy? I refuse it.

RÜDIGER: You refuse the will of the emperor? You would prefer transport by jailer's wagon to the capital of Lax, there to stand trial for attempted murder?

Wilhelmina falls to her knees.

WILHELMINA: Your Majesty.

RÜDIGER: Humility becomes you, Your Grace. Would that you displayed it more frequently. My queen, accept you this donation?

BENEVOLENCE: In bereavement, yes. I shall promptly eliminate the tolls within them, for it does not become a nation to earn its wealth from others' toil. [*Aside*] The emperor has no feeling for our grief, but constraints on trade raise his bile. Nor would Montagne object to more land 'twixt it and this.

RÜDIGER: This tragedy is concluded. We depart now with our circus, for word has reached us that the Globe d'Or awaits us in the fair city of Rigorus with a remarkably new operator, a young woman of no small skill . . . You must attend our next performance, Your Majesty . . .

Exit Rüdiger and Benevolence. Roger embraces Wisdom's coffin.

WILHELMINA: Observe His Grace. He prefers a silent wife to a speaking mother; such is the gratitude of sons.

ROGER: O Wisdom! I lodge myself before you; never will we part, my sweet!

From the Desk

of the

Queen Mother of Montagne,

& Her Cat

My Dearest Temperance, Queen of Montagne,

Well, Granddaughter, Rüdiger IV (or as I now prefer to think of him, "Rüdiger the Just") has departed for Rigorus with all his entourage, and such an event it was; the parade required an hour to pass through Froglock, with much cheering on the part of the residents, who are apparently yet ignorant of the fact that the duchy's wealth will henceforth be derived from its own citizenry.

As the whole empire knows, Rüdiger has resented for decades Farina's tolls and their deleterious effect on imperial trade;

the promise that these fees would be eliminated — combined with his discovery of a uniquely accomplished and fearless operator for his precious Globe d'Or — rendered the man positively giddy. He was equally delighted by the theatrics of the marriage ceremony, and he himself (as we plotted in my suite that fateful night, Dizzy producing handfuls of fire to impress His Majesty and Tips) suggested the curtain behind which Dizzy, once separated from her Doppelschläferin, might hide, and the hat toss to distract the audience during that crucial moment of separation.

Even as his great train of performers and accountants moved through the streets, the emperor sat in a tête-à-tête with that peculiar little Booted Maestro (sporting yet another monstrous plumed hat), the two of them calculating how best to put to use Tips and Violet. Needless to say, a circus is the ideal venue for your sister. I remain in awe of her brilliance, to deduce in a moment the magical foundation of the Globe d'Or — she has never been so clever, but then she has never in her life been so motivated! To be honest, Princess Wisdom would have made a truly dreadful ruler, particularly chafing under Wilhelmina's ungodly thumb: the good folk of Farina should count their blessings that they are left instead with her double. Let us hope that Violet has a long and delightful career with the wondrous Circus Primus, and at the end of each day finds herself crowned only in the transient glory of laurels.

Wilhelmina (I should not gossip so, but I cannot resist) for the duration of the emperor's visit treated him with the most limited civility, begging off every dinner on account of illness — as Rüdiger whispered to me one night, her clipped feathers must be paining her dreadfully! Paining her and others, I'm afraid, for the woman has sequestered herself with that miserable little dog, which bites every unfortunate soul forced to enter her chambers. Would that Escoffier were yet present to drive the beast to distraction!

Through rank, jargon, and ire, I have managed to convince the sawbones yet employed in awakening your "sister" that however they treat my granddaughter, they cannot actually *touch* her; this has put an end to talk of leeches, scouring, purges, draughts, and whatever other quackery doctors will devise for a fee. In this process I was quite assisted by Roger, who displays an endearing devotion to his stricken bride. I suspect that the duke, perhaps only instinctually, flaunts his marital commitment to irritate his mother, which it most certainly does. He has never spoken in Wilhelmina's defense, and it may be that even he suspects her of poisoning Wisdom — given the conniving he has observed throughout his life, he would have no reason to think otherwise — and seeks to communicate his disapproval by treating his bride with the ardor of Pygmalion. However long Violet continues her circus adventure, rest assured that her Doppelschläferin will be safe.

That said, their marriage is not a little monotonous, as is the court as a whole. I fear I have spent far too much of every day asleep, enjoying my Doppelschläferin exchanges with Escoffier. Life in Chateau de Montagne, even through a cat's eyes, is far more scintillating than in this stodgy palace. Had I known the Doppelschläferin spell could operate at such a distance — across nations and through mountains! — I would have put it to use far earlier, though Escoffier is doubtless quite relieved this revelation came so late.

We are both of us, Escoffier and I, observing with the greatest delight your blossoming camaraderie with sweet Trudy. She is one of the kindest, truest people I have ever known, and I am relieved beyond measure that you now have such a trust-worthy advisor at your elbow. You are the first in six genera-tions, I believe, to have been gifted with a counselor to the throne. How silly I was not to have recognized that Trudy's sight might serve a greater purpose than stopping spills and wielding buckets!

Your confidence and composure grow daily, my dear, and I cannot ascribe all or even most of this to your new friend. Painful as it may be, hardship tempers us as heat tempers steel; you have emerged from your personal inferno stronger and wiser than ever. I cannot wait to convey this in person; now that Dizzy is safe and negotiations between Farina and

Lax are complete (and Montagne firmly in possession of both Bridgeriver and Alpsburg, which shall ease my journey immeasurably!), I can return home. Until then, please accept Escoffier's affection as surrogate for my own.

Your enchanted grandmother,
Ben

Postscriptum: Teddy darling, if you manage to discover any other spies, please lock them up for my return; I shall turn them into frogs.

THE IMPERIAL ENCYCLOPEDIA
OF LAX

8TH EDITION

Printed in the Capital City of Rigorus
by Hazelnut & Filbert, Publishers to the Crown

ROGER OF FARINA

True to his word, the duke remained faithful to Wisdom, spending part of each day with his insensate bride, who lay preserved in a coffin of glass. While not abandoning outright his rule of Farina, he made no effort to conceal his disinterest in affairs of state, particularly taxation and military conquest, and often spoke of the lessons he had garnered from Wisdom's Kiss. The situation degenerated to such a degree that Wilhelmina secretly offered the throne to her youngest son, Hrothgar, then a soldier on the northern frontier and recently married himself to Colonel Ivan von Umlaut. Hrothgar did not answer Wilhelmina's proposition (he once boasted that the secret to happiness lay in never opening his mother's mail), and Roger remained duke. The dowager duchess died soon thereafter, of sepsis from an untreated dog bite, and was posthumously dubbed Wilhelmina the Ogress by her many victims. Thus unfettered, Roger erected on the palace grounds a memorial to Wisdom that soon became a pilgrimage site for local sweethearts. It is today the most popular shrine to love in all of Lax. He later took to collecting china figurines, and in response porcelain manufacturers developed a line of princesses-in-repose commonly known as Rogerware. Following Roger's death without issue in Year 47 of the reign of Rüdiger IV, the Farina courts rejected the claims of Hrothgar's adopted children as a violation of the ducal line, and so the duchy passed via Wisdom to the Kingdom of Montagne. The princess, after twenty years of unconsciousness, returned to life soon after and retired to Chateau de Montagne with a friend. Roger's figurine collection formed the seminal installation of the Farina Museum of Fine Art.

Memoirs

OF THE

Master Swordsman

FELIS EL GATO

Impresario Extraordinaire ✦ Soldier of Fortune
Mercenary of Stage & Empire

LORD OF THE LEGENDARY

FIST OF GOD

Famed Throughout the Courts and Countries of the World

&

The Great Sultanate

✳ THE BOOTED MAESTRO ✳

WRITTEN IN HIS OWN HAND ~ALL TRUTHS VERIFIED~
ALL BOASTS REAL

A Most Marvelous Entertainment,
Not to Be Missed!

VIOLET, inspired on that fateful Montagne morning to ma-
neuver the Globe d'Or that she might rescue her new companion Tomas, soon became so adept at its operation that she
eschewed the brazier altogether and managed the Globe d'Or
by some other fashion, the details of which remain vague to me,

but then, I am an artist, not a technician. With such skill she grew into one of the most valued members of Circus Primus, and her onstage pairing with Tomas soon blossomed into off-stage romance. Together they dazzled audiences in countries fourscore or more. Yet even the glow of circus spotlights dims with time; then came word that Roger, Duke of Farina, had passed, this news inexplicably dealing Violet a devastating blow. She died soon thereafter, and in his grief Tomas quit the circus to withdraw to Montagne, where I am told he reunited with the miraculously revived Princess Wisdom . . .

I myself, the modest recipient of awards past counting—a knighthood, a barony sans manorial rights, three honorary university degrees, and a carpet of alleged magical properties—after a glorious and acclaimed career retired to an expansive country estate, where I now enjoy myself immeasurably. Recently an itinerant storyteller paid a visit to my abode, and for several days I delighted him with my adventures. Curiously, he begged in particular for stories of a cat belonging to an elderly queen of Montagne. Though I barely remembered the beast, I endeavored as best I could to elaborate on my few recollections of the beast's insignificant contribution—vastly different from my own critical role in that epic!—to the great drama of Wisdom's Kiss. I chuckled anew at his battle of wits with that ferocious little dog of Duchess Wilhelmina, and at the cat's assistance in Tomas's defeat of the fiendish gardener.

At last my visitor confessed the truth: he was no wandering raconteur but rather a professional scholar of *fairy stories*, and having heard many versions of this *cat tale*—and of my own saga I am proud to admit, for it is a saga well worth gleaning—had recently, in different villages in several lands, been presented with an amalgam of the two. I begged that he relate this new account, and though reluctant at last he agreed. It was, I grant, delightful in its own simple way, if lacking the grand drama and scope of my life, though as he pointed out, my countless exploits could scarce fit between the pages of a picture book meant for children! And, while my name in that tale has been altered, I am perspicacious enough to recognize that the pseudonym is both more sensible and more fantastic, as are the details—an honest *miller's son*, his *two greedy brothers, the love of a princess*, the acquisition of a *prosperous country* ruled by an *ogre* who is conquered by *cunning*, and above all a *wise feline advisor*.

So it is that while this tome you now read shall be the definitive history of my life, I have a second biography as well, one that shines in the reflected glory of my own penning. In honor of that slight but pleasing fairy tale, I humbly sign these memoirs in that name.

With cheerful thoughts of my readers' wholesale satisfaction at this tale.

Your humble servant,
Puss in Boots

A Glossary of

One-and-Twenty Unusual Words

Found in *Wisdom's Kiss*

ABDICATION (ab•duh•KAY•shun) [From Latin *ab-*, "away" + *dicare*, "proclaim"] The formal renouncement of one's royal position; monarchal resignation. Often forced upon an unwilling ruler after a loss or a scandal, abdication has historically been rare—too rare, given the incompetence of so many kings. The word today also describes any failure of duty: "Mrs. Franklin abdicated her maternal obligations by leaving her infants in the care of a golden retriever."

ACUMEN (ACK•you•men) [From Latin *acuere*, "to sharpen"] Shrewdness; good judgment. Someone savvy with plants has horticultural acumen. *Acuere* is also the root of *acute*, as in "severe, critical, or sharp."

ARBOREAL (ar•BOR•e•al) [From Latin *arbor*, "tree"] *Arboreal* literally means "tree-ish" and refers mostly to animals, such as arboreal frogs.

DÉCOLLETAGE (day•CULL•taj) [From French *de* + *collet,* "decollar"] Décolletage describes the low neckline of a woman's dress and, implicitly, the skin that said neckline reveals. A proper-sounding word for a fairly improper subject.

DOPPELSCHLÄFERIN (dopp•ul•SHLAY•fer•in; rhymes with "topple SLAY fair in") *Doppelgänger,* German for "double goer," describes someone's real or fictitious double: "Jason fancied himself Sherlock Holmes's doppelgänger as he set out to solve the theft." The mock term Doppelschläferin, or "double female sleeper," derives from this literary term.

DOWAGER (DOW•uh•ger) A *dowry* was the property that a bride brought to her marriage. A *dower,* on the other hand, was the property that a bride and groom agreed she would receive should he die first. The dower could include the dowry (in other words, the bride would get her own family's property back) and other holdings as well, including land or a title. Thus, a woman receiving a dower was a *dowager*: a widow controlling property inherited from her dead spouse. These days, however, the word *dowager* is used to describe any older, dignified woman.

EAVESDROPPER (EVES•drop•er) *Eavesdrop* is an extinct Middle English term for the land closest to a house, the area onto which water from the eaves would drop. Someone lurking within this eavesdrop might readily overhear conversations, particularly given the quality of home construction in medieval England, and the lurker came to be known as an eavesdropper. It's a pity the original definition of eavesdrop fell out of favor, as there isn't another word for the two or three feet of soil abutting a building's foundation.

EL DORADO (el•door•AH•doe) "The Golden One" or "Gilded One" in Spanish, El Dorado was a mythical country or city of gold sought by the Spanish conquistadors, who ended up finding the Amazon River instead. It has since come to denote an often illusory place or destination of great wealth.

ENCEINTE (ehn•SAINT) [From Latin *incingere*, "to gird in"] *Enceinte* means both "a fortified enclosure" (or the wall itself) and "pregnant"; both senses are archaic. English has few tasteful terms for pregnancy, probably because pregnancy was considered too vulgar to discuss in polite company. (The Victorians, for example, referred to a woman's *confinement,* which sounds like she was in prison, though prison at least would have been better than the death that concluded far too many Victorian pregnancies.) *Enceinte* has the added advantage of being so obscure that most listeners probably wouldn't know it and would be too intimidated by its Frenchness to ask.

ENSORCELLED (en•SOR•seld) [From French *sorcier,* "sorcerer"] Enchanted; the verb *ensorcel* can mean "to bewitch" and also "to fascinate."

FORTITUDE (FOR•tih•tude) Courage in the face of adversity or pain. *Fortitude, fortress,* and *fortify* all derive from the strapping Latin *fortis,* or "strong"; a student's forte (FOR•tay), or strength, might be spelling, naptime, or gym. *Fortitude* implies emotional strength: one has courage to enter a fistfight, but fortitude to resist the taunting.

LADY-IN-WAITING A lady-in-waiting was an attendant—usually well-born herself, and most definitely not a servant, thus not paid—to a princess or a queen. A lady-in-waiting might be a trustworthy relative who served as a confidante, or a noblewoman who took the position as a form of title. Depending on the country, era, and individuals involved, a lady-in-waiting might be expected to accompany her lady on her travels, to serve ceremonial functions at public events, or to perform such tasks as writing letters, sewing, dancing, or performing music.

MELANCHOLIA (mell•un•COAL•e•a) [From Greek *melan*, "black" + khole, "bile"] Profound sadness; historically, depression. From ancient times until well into the nineteenth century, physicians believed that four fluids, or *humors,* controlled the human body. These four fluids—*phlegm* (phlegm)*, sanguine* (blood)*, choler* (yellow bile), and *melancholy* (black bile)—bore a corresponding mood: impassive (phlegmatic), optimistic (sanguine), angry (choleric), and depressed (melancholic), emotional descriptors that are still in use today—although without the leeches, vomiting, and purges that traditionally accompanied treatment of the cardinal humors. The concept that one's humors affected disposition evolved into the notion that *humor* meant "mindset" or "inclination"—"My boss was in a foul humor today"—and from there the idea that humoring someone would improve their mood. Thus the modern definition of *humor* as "amusement" or "comedy."

MOSSBACK [American] Originally a large, old fish; during the Civil War, a man who fled to avoid conscription by the Confederate army, implicitly hiding until his back sprouted moss. It now denotes any narrow-minded or old-fashioned person.

MYCOLOGY (my•COLL•uh•gy) [From Greek *mukes,* "mushroom"] The scientific study of fungi.

SAGACITY (sa•GAS•it•ee) [From Latin *sagire,* "to discern quickly or keenly"] *Sagacity* originally meant "good sense" as in "sense of smell": a sagacious hound. It has since evolved into "good sense" as in "shrewdness" or "judgment": a sagacious advisor. Oddly, the word has no relation to the similar descriptor *sage* (SAJE), which derives from the Latin *sapere,* "to be wise" (also a root of *Homo sapiens*).

SANG-FROID (sang-FRA) [From French *sang,* "blood" + *froid,* "cold"] Cold-blooded or, more aptly, cool-headed. Someone with sang-froid displays composure in the face of adversity or danger. The word is not necessarily a compliment: sometimes a little emotion—empathy, say—is very much what the situation requires.

SILVICULTURE (SIL•ve•cull•chure), or SYLVICULTURE [From Latin *silva,* "wood," + *cultura,* "cultivation"] The cultivation of trees; forestry. It is akin to agriculture [from Latin *agri,* "field"], the science of farming, and horticulture [from *hortus,* "garden"], the science of gardening.

SLATTERNLY (SLAT•urn•ly) [Archaic] Untidy, messy. A *slattern* was a messy, dirty woman, by implication a loose woman, and derived from the obsolete, wonderfully descriptive verb *slatter,* meaning "to splash or spill."

TEMPERANCE (TEM•pur•ence) Moderation, especially in regard to drinking and eating; alternatively and just as commonly, complete abstention from alcohol. During the nineteenth and early twentieth centuries, the American temperance movement at various times promoted both definitions, though the movement is most associated with the effort to end alcohol production and sales by outlawing them via prohibition. The word *temperance* derives from the Latin *temperare,* which means either "self-restraint" or "mingling"—two very different definitions each based in the concept of balance. Thus the notion that someone whose four humors (see MELANCHOLIA) were in proper proportion would be well balanced, or in a good temper.

VICTRIX (VICK•tricks) [From Latin *victor* + the feminine suffix *-ix*] A female victor. A female aviator once bore the honorific of aviatrix; a female director, directrix; a female executor, executrix. Thus, a female victor was a victrix, a victress, or even a victrice. English similarly contains the outmoded *authoress, poetess, proprietress, manageress,* and *editress.* Such words are now seen as inherently disparaging—the belittling *governess* or *mistress,* for example, compared to *governor* or *mister*—which explains why *actress, stewardess, heiress,* and *hostess* are now obsolescent, and *adulteress* is just plain goofy.

Bonus Material:

Author Commentary

Structure and Format

The Opening

Title and Cover

THE STRUCTURE AND FORMAT OF *WISDOM'S KISS*

Want to write good books? Start by writing bad screenplays.

That's been my experience, anyway, and—based on this sample of one—it's a pretty useful route to publishing. Before I tried my hand at fiction, I spent eight years studying screenwriting and learned—well, I learned everything I now know. I learned about dialogue, character development, pacing, description, plot, theme . . . However awful my screenplays ended up, I absorbed an enormous amount of information about how to make a story good, because a movie, first and foremost, is a story, and it needs to be really good because someone's spending millions of dollars to make it. (This, by the way, does not mean that the final product ends up good; many movies are terrible. But the point is that they're not terrible on purpose.)

"Three-act structure" is a bit of screenwriting jargon that for me has paid off in aces and spades. Basically it means that the first quarter ("first act") of a movie/story introduces the characters. The middle two quarters ("second act") features escalating conflict culminating in a "low point," easily identified as that depressing spot when you want to quit watching. In the last quarter ("third act") everything resolves and the hero emerges emotionally and/or physically victorious.

There: you just saved yourself eight years of screenwriting classes.

Every time I start a new book, even before I start formally

outlining the story, I pull out my screenwriting notes to review how to link the character's internal and external conflicts, how to pace the first act, et cetera, et cetera. I do this partially from superstition: given that it's worked five times, I don't want to mess with success. And it works as a writing exercise to get me thinking rather like my other favorite exercise of imagining a scene without any dialogue and then with dialogue alone . . . These processes open a lot of mental doors. But I also do it because the three-act structure really does work, and my stories are stronger for it.

When I outline a story, I translate the three acts into four columns, each representing one quarter of the book. Sometimes this four-column format makes it all the way to the final product: *Princess Ben* has four parts; *Front and Center* has sixteen chapters (16 = 4 x 4). *Wisdom's Kiss* has four parts too. (Part I includes the Introduction.) Part III, entitled "All is Lost!" is particularly notable—those are the exact words I wrote on my original outline to remind myself that this is the low point. But it's also the point of storytelling generally, a perfect summation of our craft: create conflict; then resolve it. All is lost . . . but not really.

The *Wisdom's Kiss* format, as I discuss in my commentary on Tips, Trudy, Dizzy, Ben, Felis, *The Imperial Encyclopedia of Lax*, and heavens knows where else, came about because I wanted a story told from three points of view. Almost immediately I realized that three points of view wouldn't be enough, that the story had facts and incidents and experiences that three voices alone couldn't manage. It's akin to a football game told only from the perspective of the place kicker; adding the stories of a coach and a ref and a fan would add immeasurably to our understanding. I could have pulled back and told the whole story in third person, the way a football game is told in a newspaper, but I would then lose the intimacy and emotional intensity of those personal perspectives, and lose as well the suspense. If a narrator doesn't know what's going to happen next, then the reader doesn't know either. Or the reader might know a little bit from another narrator, or know the wrong thing. That mystery feeds the dramatic tension. Dramatic tension is the gold ring. Dramatic tension is what we're aiming for.

Thus the eight perspectives of *Wisdom's Kiss,* and all the headaches and challenges and nuance that eight perspectives entailed. The story needed them, but to be honest I needed them too. I enjoyed *Wisdom's Kiss* more than anything I've ever created, a satisfaction marred only rarely by the fear that no one, in the whole future of the world, would want to read it. But it was immensely, hilariously satisfying to write Dizzy's diary without commas, to make sure that only Trudy got to use the word "horrid," to puzzle out what Tips could spell and what he couldn't, and to decide whether the three entries that constitute Wilhelmina's encyclopedia biography should conclude with ellipses. The glossary was equally satisfying, though I'm surprised at how those marvelous words often came across as stuffy; writing zippy dictionary definitions is a lot harder than I'd thought. But please, please don't let that dissuade you from putting to use your own dictionary. The English language is an extraordinary achievement; think of *Wisdom's Kiss* as a present to us.

THE OPENING OF *WISDOM'S KISS*

Wisdom's Kiss began with Trudy's roadside vision of approaching menace. This is to say that *Wisdom's Kiss* began not only with this inspiration, but for a good many drafts with this as the actual opening of the book.

As an opener, it has a lot going for it. The scene introduces the reader to Trudy and her devotion to Tips; it demonstrates the power and mystery of her clairvoyance; it even shows her passion for family as she tries to protect a hen and chicks—to be sure, a singularly ungrateful hen. I also loved that "muttered fowl curses" line; anyone who's ever worked with chickens knows that warning croon.

But, sweet as it was, the scene didn't light me on fire. It didn't suck me in as the opener of a book should. (Note the first line of *The Titan's Curse,* book three of Rick Riordan's Percy Jackson and the Olympians series: "The Friday before winter break, my mom packed me an overnight bag and a few deadly weapons and took me to a new boarding school." Now *that's* an opener.)

Whenever I thought about this new *Wisdom's Kiss* book I was supposed to be writing, I'd get especially enthusiastic about Tips's diving scene. Felis's description of Tips leaping off that great mossy waterwheel and arcing into the dark water of the pond . . . It gave me goose bumps. Still does. When I sent my publisher a proposal for *Wisdom's Kiss* and needed to include a writing sample, I included *that* scene— not, you notice, the scene of Trudy and the chickens. Plus there was that whole wonderful Felis overlay, his ridiculous memoir title and vainglorious vocabulary and preening self-regard . . . This was a character I wanted to know more about, find out what this boastful little maestro intended to do with such a talented lad. Not to mention that the scene (her lookout for Tips's brother, her knowledge of that eavesdropping-free conversation) also hinted at Trudy's clairvoyance!

But. But the pluses of Felis's memoir were also its drawbacks. For every reader drawn into this succulent prose, another would be irrevocably alienated by the vocabulary. Why toss readers (as it were) into the deep end of the pool? Wouldn't it be smarter (from a marketing standpoint, yes, but also as a storyteller) to draw the reader in gently? To start in the shallow end, with floaties?

Everyone agreed that this was a problem. It wasn't—unlike some other battles I can recall, to my shame—other people telling me it didn't work and me refusing to listen. I saw it too; I just didn't know how to fix it. I also wanted a softer opening, but without sacrificing that juicy Felis extravagance.

So, thinking cap jammed tightly on skull, I ruminated away . . . and thus remembered a scene I'd envisioned very early in the outlining process, well before I touched pen to paper. (Okay, before I put fingers to keyboard.) While pondering Trudy's sight, I'd tried to figure out when it first happened, and came up with the idea of a small child inadvertently discovering a villain. It was a great character-development exercise, but as far as the book went, it didn't really work; it would mean beginning the story a decade earlier and then having to contrive one of those "ten years later, our heroes . . ." type solutions. I hate those. For me, the tighter the chronology, the better. If I could write a book that takes place over twenty-four or even two hours, I'd be thrilled. Tight = taut; stretched = saggy.

Now faced with this crisis, however, I returned to that saggy notion. Everyone who read *Wisdom's Kiss* loved Trudy and agreed she was the central character; it made absolute sense to begin the story with her. The memoir prose of *A Life Unforeseen* was far more digestible than Felis's excess. Not to mention—Oh, how I love serendipity!—that introducing Trudy and Tips as children could thus make the dive scene far more dramatic; readers would already know and empathize with this twosome.

I then spun off these two entries—Trudy's childhood plus Felis's dive story—into a separate, formal introduction and explained the six-year gap in chronology by titling Part I— creatively enough—"Six Years Later." Such is authorial flexibility. Plus the introduction's title cracks me up—I always imagine Dizzy being the one who composed it.

TITLE AND COVER

Some books have titles that leap from one's brow in the way that Athena, fully formed, leapt from the brow of Zeus. *Dairy Queen* and *Princess Ben* both fall in this category. I thought them up like this: *poof!* Everyone agreed that they were wonderful or at least tolerable. No one ever looked back.

Then there are the titles that lurk like blind, eyeless cave fish in the unlit pits of one's subconscious, refusing ever to reveal themselves. Into this latter category falls *Wisdom's Kiss*. I was most moved, while watching the movie *Julie & Julia,* by the scene in which Julia Child and her editor struggle for hours on end to come up with a title for *Mastering the Art of French Cooking*. Good gracious, I know that pain.

The original title of *Wisdom's Kiss* was "Fortitude, Wisdom and Tips," which from the get-go I knew was bad, not least because its abbreviation is far too close to one of those naughty modern acronyms. "WORKING TITLE!" I wrote on the cover, just to clarify that even the author knew it stunk. Then we started spitballing. Make any amalgam of Wisdom, Tips, Trudy, Fortitude, Cat, Magic, Air, Farina, Froglock, Misadventure and/or Adventure, Passion, Love, Gold, Whiskers—you'll come up with at least one of our suggested titles. I can't remember exactly what Julia Child/Meryl Streep says in *Julie & Julia* when they finally settle on *Mastering the Art of French Cooking*; something akin to "I'm too tired to think! Why not?" That's how I felt when we finally combined "wisdom" and "kiss": why not. (And then we had to go through the whole bloody process again with the subtitle. I'm still bummed that "oysters" didn't make it: *A Thrilling and Romantic Adventure Incorporating Magic, Oysters, Villainy, and a Cat*—isn't that fun? But there wasn't room on the page, or something.)

My feelings about the *Wisdom's Kiss* title have since blossomed from acceptance into heartfelt affection, though I confess that in my private notes I refer to it as *WisK,* mentally pronounced as "whisk." I haven't said this aloud—yet—but I will soon, and will then be regarded with justifiable disbelief. Possibly horror. To be honest, I have never viewed myself as the kind of author who writes titles featuring the word "Kiss"—kissing is a relatively minor element in my fiction—but live and learn.

Once we settled on this title, I had to go back and weave in subtle references to the phrase "Wisdom's kiss," a job I enjoyed enormously. The deleted stuff is better still.

Like a book's title, the cover art requires synthesizing a complex, multicharacter narrative into a package that will appeal to the broadest selection of readers while also conveying its most important themes and emphasizing its originality and nuance.

Good luck with that one.

But Houghton Mifflin—hands together, everyone—pulled it off. That picture of ball gown + hair + cat (there's a girl in there too, somewhere, but really it's all about the dress) blows me away. When I showed it to my sister, she gasped: "This is every picture you ever drew as a kid!" Which, oddly, I had not realized . . . Although on some level I must have because I did, you know, write the story that inspired the art. I will take credit for the cat. In an earlier, different cover version I pushed hard for a cat, feeling that it would enhance the cover's humor and quirkiness. Doubtless the designer thought of it independent of my suggestion, but I'm still content to look at that sable beauty and think, "You're mine, dude. You're all mine."

Excerpts from

Princess Ben

Being a Wholly Truthful

Account of Her Various

Discoveries and Misadventures,

Recounted to the Best of Her

Recollection, in Four Parts

Dangers of Magic

Both Ben and Dizzy are quite hesitant to employ magic, not only from the untimely death of Queen Providence but also because of the violent punishment of any practitioners, or even suspected practitioners. Nonna Ben has long experience with the hazards of both witchcraft and broom flight, as this passage (pages 150–51) demonstrates.

Oh, how I longed to soar through the sky! Past the stars, across the moon, over sleeping Montagne and its flag-adorned turrets. Even as I dreamt of this rapture, my wiser side spoke against it. Rumors of witchcraft now burned across the country. Sheep on Ancienne had gone astray; a shepherd boy had not been seen in weeks; spirits with cloven feet tracked ash across the ballroom floor. As far as the truth went, I had seen the ballroom myself, and the prints (well should I know) were only mice. Sheep had been disappearing from the mountain since time immemorial; rational men in rational times agreed the creatures must be tumbling into an unmarked ravine. As for the shepherd boy, I had no insights beyond the knowledge that I was in no way responsible.

Yet tempers were raw, and the castle's populace, tense over the impending ball and doubtless sensing in some intangible way the threat from Drachensbett, promised violence against anyone suspected of sorcery. Better to dart about my cell like a beetle trapped in a jar, and to enter the pantries only when my howling belly could bear hunger no more.

BEN'S MISBEHAVIOR

Trudy may believe that doughty Queen Ben has behaved perfectly all her life, but readers of Princess Ben *know better. Here (pages 55–57), Ben describes her experience as a newly crowned, fifteen-year-old princess-in-training.*

Much of each day I passed in the company of Lady Beatrix, a tall and bony woman of unknowable age who never appeared without a wig and a thick spackling of powder, rouge, and lipstick, a mole painted somewhere between her cheekbone and chin depending on the formality of the occasion. As an educator, she was utterly lacking.

Her notion of history centered on genealogy, emphasizing Queen Sophia's superior bloodlines. Though she spoke several languages, her vocabulary consisted of fashion and dining terms and fawning, useless phrases. Because she insisted on teaching me three tongues at once, I eventually uttered such nonsense as "the draperies in this hall are lovely," but in a tangle of languages and grammar that not even she could unravel. Penmanship I found equally wretched, for I had far less interest in the appearance of my words than in their substance, a concept that held no meaning for my teacher. . . .

Needlework—oh, hateful needlework! How many loathsome hours did I spend embroidering handkerchiefs with ridiculous flowers and illegible initials, only for Beatrix to reject them. "Someday," she would simper, "a prince himself will request your handkerchief as token. This would be shameful to present."

"I don't care about tokens!" I snapped. "I don't care about princes, either!" I found it effortless to talk back to her, but ultimately unsatisfying, as she ignored me utterly.

"Remember, Benevolence," she would say, handing me another square of linen, "'Tis a needle, not a lance. Gentle stitches."

Dance and music were taught by stout little Monsieur Grosbouche, whose hands were as cold and damp as freshly caught fish. He, too, believed that the promise of well-born bachelors should inspire my greatest exertions. As he dragged me through each minuet, polonaise, and gavotte, puffing the beat with odiferous breath, I entertained myself by stepping on the wide bows of his high-heeled dance slippers, then sweetly awaiting his stumble.

ELEMENTAL SPELLS

Nonna Ben first discovered the Elemental Spells as a sullen and lonely teenager, the same night she stumbled upon the secret Wizard Room. As her memoir Princess Ben *relates (pages 90–92) mastery of the Elemental Spells was fitful at best, and Ben's intentions were often less than admirable.*

If I had not yet come to the conclusion that this tome was a force of magic, the title words—difficult to discern, for the room though illuminated by the moon had not light for scholarship—left no doubt. "The Elemental Spells," they proclaimed, in a flowing, archaic script I would discover soon enough was not the easiest to decipher. A dense paragraph followed, too challenging to read in the weak light, and then a series of precise illustrations and captions, with arrows highlighting specific elements, much as a cookery book might demonstrate the proper way to trim a roast, or an engineering manual the ideal configuration of a gristmill . . .

. . . Beneath [each] drawing was a series of words in a tongue I did not recognize; it looked wild, foreign, and unpronounceable. Helpfully, a second line of text sounded the words out syllable by syllable. . . .

Across the two pages, I could see now, every chain of pictures ended with cupped hands, and each set of hands held a different substance. One clutched a lump resembling soil, another water with rippling surface. The third pair held what could only have been fire, sans a single indication of discomfort. The last hands I puzzled over, for they appeared to harbor a puff of mist, much like the clouds forever swirling about the base of our waterfall. These pictures meant something, I knew, but what?

Suddenly, as I scanned the pages' title, it struck me. The elemental spells these were, and such they produced: the four elements of earth, water, fire, and air.

What good such spells would accomplish I had not a clue. The ability to make dirt, or air, seemed rather a waste of magic. Fire, however, particularly a flame one could hold without danger—that was a different situation altogether.

DOPPELSCHLÄFERIN

I invented this word (see the Wisdom's Kiss *glossary) while reworking* Sleeping Beauty *for my fairy tale* Princess Ben; *in creating a magical spell that allows someone to split in two, I retitled and feminized it as "double sleeper," thus finally putting to use two miserable years of college German. But since pretty much no one can pronounce German, let alone understand it, this name ended up as yet another Catherine Murdock linguistic dud. Plus it's impossible to type. German is notorious for huge, unwieldy words: in only our second week of college, we were memorizing "speed limit":* Geschwindigkeitbegrenzung. *"Doppelschläferin" is nothing compared with that.*

In this excerpt (pages 105–11), Ben discovers the Doppelschläferin in a book of magical spells. Note that this description does not feature the use of a cat as a body double; I hadn't figured out that part yet.

The illustrations made no sense. A girl under pursuit drops to the ground and perishes, for a ghost steps from her body. Her pursuers gather about the corpse as the ghost slips away unnoticed. Later the ghost reappears and steps, as one would descend a staircase, into the corpse, which then returns to life. Inserted between these larger images were diagrams of hand gestures and phonetic phrasing of spells.

A body returned to life was black magic; that much I knew. Perhaps the presence in this wizard room was not so benevolent after all. Even the heavy Gothic script of the title unnerved me.

Wondering what path of villainy I might even now be treading, I sounded the name out, struggling with the foreign pronunciation: "Die Doppelschläferin." Beneath this, I could espy, smaller but in the same heavy text, "The Sleeping Double." . . .

. . . [Ah!] The girl in the wizard room's spell had avoided her pursuers by splitting herself in twain, the sleeping portion serving as distraction while the more active half went about her business. I had not pursuers per se, but I suffered myriad prying and suspicious opponents. I had escaped the queen's wrath once; I might not be so fortunate again. I, too, required a sleeping double to remain in the cell while I occupied myself without distraction above. I determined to spend all night, if need be, mastering the Doppelschläferin.